Will's War in Exile

By Nisse Visser

CONTENTS

1. Leaving Brighton

Will Maskall leant against the wrought iron railings as he looked out over the sea. He was thirteen years old. His threadbare shorts and thin light blue wool jumper betrayed that he hailed from the slums. His blond hair was unkempt and in need of a cut, although a thick bandage wrapped around his head explained this apparent oversight.

To Will's right the sun was beginning to sink towards Brighton's rooftops, soon to be starkly outlined in black as the horizon transformed into a spectacle of red and pink hues. Overhead seagulls floated in wide lazy circles uttering forlorn cries. The starlings had ventured to the seafront from their usual inland haunts and were in full murmuration. They formed a black cloud which spiralled in a graceful dance over the sea, occasionally weaving over and around Palace Pier.

These sights were pillars of Will's grasp on existence. They had always been there, different and the same; always fascinating and beautiful.

Other such certainties had been taken away. Madeira Drive, far below his vantage point on Marine Parade, was now inaccessible. It had been Will's favourite haunt on the seafront. He had got used already to the mass entanglements of barbed wire, concrete blocks and the stakes pointing out to sea to ward off invasion craft. Just like the sand-bagged machine gun posts and artillery positions on Marine Parade and King's Road had become a familiar sight.

When these things had been installed Will had felt as if part of Brighton had been stolen from him. It had taken time for him to understand that the eccentric old lady he called home had merely once again transformed her face to wear the sign of the times in her own peculiar charming manner.

The boy drank it all in, his mind in a whirl for now even the absolute sureties of his life – the crash, rattle and hiss of the waves pounding the shingle beach, Palace Pier and West Pier outlined in a Brighton sunset, the starlings and gulls, the magnificence and the squalor which fused into one delightful whole – were about to disappear from his life. Where would that leave him? The future seemed filled with uprooted despair.

An old man approached the boy. He did so slowly not because he was infirm but because he suspected Will was saying goodbye to his home town.

"Your Mum and Gammer are fretting, lad." The old man said when he reached the boy.

Will Maskall nodded at his grandfather: "I am sorry Gaffer; should have said I was going for a walk."

"You did Will, you did." Gaffer chuckled. "About four hours ago. I reckoned I would find you on the seafront. It's getting chilly, I brought your coat."

Will grinned uncertainly. Time had been playing tricks on his mind ever since he had come to in a ward of the Royal Sussex County Hospital; passing by interminably slow or rushing ahead to leave him floundering in its wake. A lot of daytime things seemed unreal like a confusing dream, and his nighttime dreams were filled with war-torn horrors.

"Gaffer, I don't want to leave. I turned thirteen last week, I am nearly grown."

"I understand, truly I do." The old man said. "But 'want' and 'need' are at odds here. You need to leave lad, be elsewhere for a while. Some place safer. Come, let's go back to Carlton Hill."

Will nodded morosely and followed his grandfather across Marine Parade and then into Kemptown. The palatial seaside elegance made way for more modest residences in the side streets and shops as they crossed over St James Street and Edward Street. By the time they were making their way up John Street the houses on either side of the street had become smaller and bereft of ornamental decoration.

As always Will looked towards his left as they passed the Kingswood Flats. The residential complex had been completed a few years before as part of a slums clearing programme and to Will their rounded stairwells looked like castle towers. He was also fascinated by the complex web of pipes and drains which clung to the walls; they had running water and inside toilets in the flats, an unheard of luxury on Carlton Hill.

Somebody was standing on the top gallery and upon a second surprised look Will determined that it really was a clown; wearing a flowered bowler hat atop a curly wig and red face paint on his cheeks and around his mouth. The clown waved and the boy waved back, daring a little smile even at the unexpected sight.

"Eric!" The clown suddenly called, and Gaffer looked up, his face cracking in a broad grin when he saw who called him.

The clown rushed along the gallery and disappeared into one of the round towers.

"That's Tom, one of my mates from the pub," Gaffer explained to Will who was marvelling at hearing his grandfather's christian name.

They made their way back to the main entrance of the complex on the corner of John Street and Kingswood Street and saw the clown spill out of the flats and amble towards them like a duck because of his elongated multi-coloured shoes. Will grinned at the sight.

"Were you having fun at a party, Tom?" Gaffer grinned as he shook the clown's hand. "This is my grandson, Will."

"I was working Eric. Horrible, no fun at all, they thought I was a clown. Tommy Tickle, at your service young man." The clown bowed and then widened his face in mock horror as wig and hat came tumbling off. He deftly caught them and put them back, albeit front to back so that his eyes and nose were screened by the wig. "You didn't just see this happen, young man. You have no evidence and it will be your word against mine. Judges find me highly credible, so they do."

Will laughed and waited for the clown to re-adjust his hat and wig. The man didn't, turning to Gaffer instead.

"One egg! One egg, Eric!" The clown exclaimed, his voice full of outrage.

Gaffer nodded. "Aye, rations are hard."

"One egg! It's all I am allowed a week. I like to eat a score of them for breakfast." The clown adjusted his wig and hat at last and he looked at Will now. "Two score!"

"Seven days a week," Will nodded his agreement, he liked eggs and disliked the rations which left him feeling hungry more often than not.

"He's clever!" The clown was delighted. "You've got a clever lad here Eric, well done. Though…" the clown's face fell to one which conveyed deep sadness, "…tis a curse just as much as it's a blessing."

"Aye, so it is," Gaffer agreed.

"An egg!" The clown raised a finger and smiled happiness. The boy was fascinated by the rapid transformation of facial expressions and eagerly awaited whatever would come next.

The clown's face changed to one of utter tragedy. "One egg, and I break it! I break my one egg, Eric! Will!" The clown took out a polka-dotted handkerchief and blew his nose with elephantic exaggeration.

Will laughed.

"You think it's funny?" The clown pouted. "This is a real-life story of infinitely tragic proportions. Are you cruel? Is something wrong with you?"

"Give the lad a break," the old man said. "None of us know when you are serious and when you ain't, Tom."

"Precisely!" The clown gave the boy an encouraging pat on the shoulders. "Choose your profession well, son. I made a mess of it. Everybody takes me seriously when I clown about and think I am clowning when I try to be serious. Tis a curse. I blame the seagulls."

Will was uncertain how to respond, so tried to steer the conversation back to things he understood. "Eggs are good though."

The clown beamed. "Yes! Clever lad, lesson learnt, you passed your exam."

"Well, you've made the lad smile, first smile in days." Gaffer said.

"You're sad?" The clown peered at the boy. "Of course you are sad, I should have seen that for a clown is the opposite of what he portrays and we know sadness intimately."

Will shrugged. "I am to be evacuated. Out of Brighton. Into the countryside."

"Sadness galore! Sadness galore!" The clown nodded. "Brighton will need bright young men such as yourself after the war. Stay safe and then come back home. Sounds like a sound plan to me."

"Erm, alright," Will agreed, as he had little choice in the matter anyhow.

"And," the clown captured the boy's eyes with his own. "Don't lose yourself out there, lad. Always remember who you are. But don't be afraid to change either, you'll still be you even if you change beyond all recognition."

Will nodded uncertainly, not making sense of the clown's words but committing them to memory anyway, because he sensed there might be some wisdom in them.

§ § § § § § §

The platform at Brighton Station was crowded and Will wandered away, to the front of the train, to escape the groups of children and parents milling about in front of the carriages. Some of the children were teary-eyed, others excitedly happy. Will himself had sunk into indifference. Having accepted that he could not evade evacuation, he had become listless and bereft of purpose. The one thing which awoke his interest was the locomotive. Despite the fact that it would facilitate his exile from Brighton, Will could still appreciate the raw power it exuded. Though motionless, its innards rumbled as if it were in need of feeding and it hissed out jets of steam around its great many spoked wheels.

Gaffer followed Will. Mum had to work and it was Gaffer who brought Will to the station, uncharacteristically fussy like Mum and Gran tended to be, making sure Will still had his evacuee label around his neck multiple times and keeping track of the boy's gasmask box and various items of luggage.

"You have the letter to your great uncle Maskall safely put away?" Gaffer asked for the umpteenth time.

"Yes, Gaffer," Will answered patiently, though he suddenly wanted the parting to be over with.

"Do remember to give it to him, he sent a telegram to say you would be picked up at Nickleby station."

Will nodded. These instructions too were a repetition.

Nickleby. Where on earth was this place and who had made up such a strange name? He knew the farm he was supposed to go to wasn't in Nickleby, but near another unknown place called Wolfden.

A shrill whistle pierced the buzz of noise on the platform, followed by a loud: "ALL ABOARD!"

Will felt dead inside.

"Will…" Gaffer said, biting his lip. For a moment Will was afraid there would be a hug. Part of him wanted that hug, to hide in Gaffer's firm embrace, but if he was expected to bear the punishment of exile in a grown-up manner then he wanted to be treated as such. Gaffer seemed to understand and reached out his hand. "Make the most of it, lad."

Will shook his grandfather's hand. "You take care of Mum and Gran, please."

Gaffer nodded and then helped Will lift his various belongings through the door of a seating compartment in the first carriage. Most of the evacuees were further to the back of the train and the carriage was relatively empty, although children began to trickle in as they made their way forwards through the busy train. Will lifted his Tommy helmet and set it on his head, although it was more ill-fitting than ever in combination with the bandage around Will's head and its weight pressed on the tender part of his skull behind his ear where the shrapnel had been removed.

Will could hear the locomotive start to chug, seemingly haphazard at first but then with increasing rhythmical confidence and then the train jolted into motion. Gaffer waved and Will waved back, stretching his neck to see his grandfather on the platform as the train pulled out of the station. It passed underneath the intricate web of curved steel arches that supported the curved roof and chugged into a dull but dry day. There were a few parents around Gaffer but he seemed a lonely and forlorn figure nonetheless. Will would miss him.

Brighton appeared as a choppy sea of rooftops and Will scanned the view from the window, overcome by the understanding that it would be his last view of the town for some time. He marvelled at the familiar landmarks and tried to get his head around the notion it might be months before he would see them again. Identifying known and favourite corners of the town though, also brought him vivid memories of his best mate Jamie. The knowledge that Jamie would never roam those streets again hit him hard and robbed the sights of their familiarity, almost reducing Brighton to a cold stranger. Sinking into a morose sense of hopelessness, Will barely registered the compartment's door opening until two children stepped into his view.

A girl with short mousy hair wearing a red coat and clutching – along with her bags – a large doll with a cracked porcelain face, and a little boy with dark curly hair clutching a blue and white stuffed rabbit.

"Hullo Will," the girl said cheerfully, and then started depositing her things before sitting down. The little boy followed suit without taking his large curious eyes off the older boy. Will knew them well enough. Brenda and Eddie had been Jamie's neighbours and occasionally involved in play. Brenda was about nine, Will thought, and drawn in because five-year-old Eddie loved the rough and tumble of the games Jamie and Will used to play.

"Oh, hello," Will said wearily. He had rather hoped to stew in his misery by himself, not sure if it was wise to attach himself to people who might be taken away by the war with no notice other than the rattle of machine guns or the whistling of a falling bomb.

"So where are they sending you?" Brenda peered at his label but appeared to have trouble reading it.

"I have to get off at a place called Nickleby," Will said glumly and looked outside again at the last rooftops of Brighton which were passing by.

"Oh," Brenda said. "Eddie and I are to get out at a place called Odesby. I think that's one station further along from Nickleby. Exciting isn't it?"

Will looked at her, disbelieving her cheer and then he admonished himself for being so gloomy. Departure from Brighton could hardly be a cheerful prospect for any of the other children either.

10

"Spitfire?" Eddie asked, casting longing looks at the large wood airplane model Will clutched in one hand. It had been lovingly constructed and painted by Mr Hall, Jamie's dad.

Will hesitated for a moment.

"Just be real careful with it, alright? It was Jamie's," he said.

Eddie nodded eagerly, very gingerly taking hold of the toy as Will handed it over with some reluctance.

"If you break it I shall toss Buntings out of the train window and the foxes will eat him," Brenda said.

Will grinned a little when he saw how serious Eddie took that threat. The little boy nodded somewhat downcast but was clearly delighted to be holding the beautiful toy Spitfire.

"I do hope we will be sent to nice people," Brenda said brightly, though Will suspected the happy tone was fabricated for the benefit of her little brother.

"You mean you don't know?" Will asked, surprised until he recalled not everyone had distant relatives in the countryside willing to take them in. He supposed he was luckier than some in that respect.

"Of course not, we will be told at Odesby," Brenda mirrored his surprise. "Do you know?"

"My great uncle. He lives on a farm somewhere north of Nickleby." Will's spirit sank again.

"A farm! How nice," Brenda said.

"I have never met him, nor been at a farm," Will looked out the window again and then briefly flared into frustration. "Someone told me not to lose myself there but I am a Brighton boy; I have no idea what to do on a farm."

"*Dig for Victory!*" Brenda exclaimed.

"*Straight from the plot to the pot!*" Will smiled, though a brief shadow flitted over his face.

"I am sure a farm will be terribly exciting," Brenda said wistfully. "Better than a town house. At a farm there is…space."

Will looked at her thoughtfully. "We'll be strangers in a strange place. Some of those evacuee children from London…"

Brenda laughed.

"Do you know the Millersons? On West Drive, by Queen's Park?" She asked.

"No," Will answered, as images of Queen's Park surfaced in his memory.

"They had two East End urchins." Brenda giggled. "They came back one afternoon and found that the boys had plucked the parrot and were cooking it in the kitchen."

Will laughed.

"We had a posh one in our class," Will grinned. "Wanted to know why we didn't play cricket at school. He used Latin words to try and sound important."

"I remember him," Brenda said. "He wasn't at school long was he?"

"After a week he blew his lid off because the family he was staying with on Windmill Street showed him how to use the tin bath. The outhouse had already shocked him. He had been…"

12

Will imitated a mock falsetto upper-class accent.

"…simply appalled, a totally appalling situation."

Brenda laughed.

"Jamie was better at doing impressions," Will said.

"Jamie was…," Brenda hesitated. "I miss him."

"So do I," Will nodded with a sad smile.

They looked at each other for a moment in mutual understanding, then the conversation moved on to other people they both knew; familiar streets, sweet shops, parks, and – of course – the seafront.

"You know," Will said. "I just hope there are…adventures. I had adventures all the time in Brighton. I don't know if you can have real adventures in the countryside."

"I am sure you can," Brenda answered without much conviction. "I just hope…"

"The people," Will answered, beginning to understand her fears. "Are you worried?"

"Yes," Brenda admitted.

Will grinned. "If this Odesby of yours is not far from my Nickleby, we should try to meet. We're both Brightonians. We're standing up to the bleeding Nazis aren't we? We should manage with the country people."

"I don't even know where I am going," she pointed out.

"True," Will nodded. "Try to get word to the Maskall Farm. That's all I know, but maybe somebody will know the name?"

"Maskall Farm," Eddie chirped.

"Yes, send word where you are. I'll come find you two, it'll be my first adventure," Will promised. "Do you want a sweet? I've got lots."

He dug around in his battered suitcase and produced an unbelievably big bag filled with sweets of all sorts. He had got them from all his neighbours after that fateful bombing raid on Kemptown. He had been meaning to save them in order to share them with Jamie during the fortnight that he had found it hard to fully comprehend that Jamie was gone forever.

There followed a learned debate about the best sorts of sweets and all manner of them were tried as the train moved north-east. There was comfort in having someone to talk to about to about familiar places and things that were being left behind and a sense that circumstances had cast them in the same boat. For a while, at least, it felt like they were friends.

The train was delayed once as it sheltered in a tunnel after a station master of a small county station had warned them raiders had been spotted in the sky. After that the journey became uneventful; the locomotive chugged industriously, spouting smoke as it pulled the carriages away from Brighton and deeper and deeper into Sussex.

2. A Nice Clean Girl

The train rolled to a stop at a station that was little more than a single platform. There was a station master's post the size of a large garden shed which rose above the platform like the superstructure of a submarine.

Will tumbled out of the train with all his belongings. He was the only one to get off at the Nickleby train station.

Brenda stood up and opened the window of the compartment door. Eddie came to stand by her. Brenda was sure there must be proper things to say at moments like these, but the goodbye was pressing on her. Somehow she had felt less orphaned while there had been a familiar face and voice to keep her mind off the uncertainty of her destination. Will was rummaging about in one of his bags and then turned to face them.

"We'll find each other," he promised.

That must have been the proper thing to say, as if they were on some marvelous adventure in the pictures.

"We'll try," Brenda said, not willing to rely on flights of fancy.

"Maskall Farm," Eddie nodded.

"Here," Will pushed the paper bag, still half full of sweets, in Eddie's hands. "It's for you, don't eat them at all once and share them with your sister."

Eddie nodded solemnly and then broke into a delighted grin as he peered in the bag.

The train driver let his whistle sound and the engine spat out clouds of steam further on up the platform.

"This is for you," Will held out his hand to Brenda who tentatively took three round pebbles from it. She held them and looked at them as she tried to figure out why Will had selected them as a parting gift. They were all roughly the same shape and size and though their colouration was pretty they were nothing but ordinary pebbles; you could find tens of thousands just like these on Brighton's shingle beaches...her face lit up and she clutched the pebbles tightly. She looked at Will with a question in her eyes. The locomotive was hissing as if to gather effort for the continuation of the journey and its engine started to chug louder.

Will nodded and had to speak up to be heard over the locomotive's din.

"In between the Halfway Station and Banjo Groyne. I got a bag full."

"A piece of Brighton," Brenda said.

"Yes, a bit of Brighton. Take good care of it."

The carriage shook into motion and Will waved goodbye. Brenda and Eddie waved back as the train pulled out of the station and kept waving until Will was just a dot on the distant platform.

Eddie sat down and started another inspection of the gifted bag of sweets while Brenda closed the window. It wouldn't do for them to catch a cold.

"Will gave me loads of sweets," Eddie enthused. "Loads and loads, look Brenda!"

"Wasn't that nice of him?" Brenda asked and patiently listened as Eddie, who had been paying keen attention to the learned discussion on sweets conducted by his big sister and Will, started naming them all.

It wasn't long afterwards that the train pulled into Odesby station, which was much larger than Nickleby's single platform, with a proper waiting room and ticket office. Two score children alighted from the train and the platform momentarily transformed into a hive of activity as luggage was checked and goodbyes were called to old and new friends who stayed on the train.

When the train chugged out of the station again to continue its journey the station felt empty and the children left on the platform instinctively drew together, many of them with anxiety on their faces. Eddie felt their worry and clutched Brenda's hand as hard as he could. They were approached by a woman with silver hair and a clipboard who introduced herself as the local billeting officer and led them out of the station and onto the street.

The street wasn't particularly busy, some lorries and a farm wagon passed by as the billeting officer arranged the children in ranks and instructed them to march eastwards. Most of the buildings along the street were workshops or storehouses. After some time Brenda could see small rows of terraced cottages but they didn't go there, instead they stopped by a school building and were directed to the playground behind it by the billeting officer. When they were neatly lined up the back doors opened and a variety of people stepped out; some dressed in suits and proper dresses, others in work clothes of one type or another.

The grown-ups wandered along the line and now and then would point at a terrified child and say: "I'll have this one."

The billeting officer would then come forwards with her clipboard and make notes. Brenda was horrified. Although she had never been to a cattle market so couldn't really draw the comparison she felt as if she had landed in the middle of one nonetheless. She cast her eyes down, trying to shield herself from prying eyes.

"I think I'll have this one," she heard a gruff voice say. "Look at me, lass."

Fighting her horror, Brenda slowly lifted her face to look at the speaker. He was a large man with scruffy overalls and wild blond-greying hair which refused to stay tucked into his working man's cap. His face, though weathered, was round and friendly.

The billeting officer joined them and checked her clipboard.

"Brenda Rodmelle, nine years old. From Brighton." She told the man. "And who are you, if I may ask?"

"Oh, Jeremy Hornsby, howsumdever, she bain't for me," the man explained. "We're housing a couple from Eastbourne on the farm and they've been assigned one juvenile Vackie. They are feeling poorly and asked me to collect a 'nice clean girl', their words, ma'am, not mine."

The man shrugged apologetically at Brenda.

Brenda shook her head. "I can't go with you."

"Nonsense, child," the billeting officer said. "You have no say in this matter, matching you up with hosts is my job."

"You don't understand," Brenda began to speak faster, feeling the beginning of a panic. "This is my brother Edward, they promised Mum we wouldn't be split up. They promised!"

Eddie sensed Brenda's growing anxiety and clutched her hand. "I want to stay with Brenda!"

"I was told to bring just the one," the man said. "'Tis unaccountable."

"*They*," the billeting officer said with pursed lips. "Do not seem to understand what it is like at this end, it is nigh impossible to keep promises made with no regard for reality."

Eddie began to wail and Brenda felt her own tears welling up. "I promised Mum," she protested. "With my hand on the Bible. I swore an oath, I am not leaving Eddie alone."

"Come on child," the billeting officer reached for Eddie's hand. "Let go of your sister."

Eddie howled and wrapped his arms around Brenda, burying his face in her side which at least muffled his anguished fears.

Realising that the billeting officer wasn't going to be much use Brenda looked at the farmer, for she supposed the man was that, with an imploring look. "Please," she whispered. "I can't leave him by himself. I promised."

"I am so sorry, Mr Hornsby," the billeting officer said nervously. "It might be better for you to pick another…"

"Naun," Mr Hornsby shook his head slowly. He turned to the billeting officer and said: "I've got three chavvies of my own, and if the situation were reversed, I'd be middling proud if any of them put up such a spirited fight to stay together. I'll take the both of them and we'll work it out back at the farm."

He turned back to Brenda and winked at her. Brenda felt relief surge through her. She felt Eddie convulse with sobs and kneeled down to wrap her arms around him.

"There Eddie, did you hear the nice man?" She said in a soothing voice. "We are going to stay together."

Eddie looked at her, pouting, his face wet with tears. "Promise?" he whispered.

"Promise," Brenda smiled at him.

To their left other children began to wail and clutch each other. The billeting officer made a quick note on her clipboard and then moved towards the new commotion.

"Let's get you out of here, lass," Mr Hornsby said. "'Tis a madhouse here and naun worthy of Sussex, sureleye."

Brenda nodded. She felt drained but gathered her belongings and with Eddie at her side she followed Mr Hornsby out of the schoolyard and away from the market scenes that were being tragically played out.

3. Ancestral Home

Will kept on waving as the train chugga-chood into the distance. When it was gone he looked up to see…

…absolutely nothing.

As far as he could see fields rolled along with the contour of the land. They were interspersed with copses of trees and hedges. He saw no buildings and no roads; just emptiness. It made him feel slightly dizzy and he took a deep breath and turned around fearing the same view. Instead of fields there were trees. A seemingly impenetrable wall of trees which stretched endlessly to his right. When he turned left he saw a similar green wall but one that ended half-a-mile away in a patchwork of fields centred by a small church around which were huddled a score of cottages.

The station master came walking out of his post. Moving towards Will slowly for he was at least two hundred years old with a bent back and spindly legs. He used a stout walking stick to aid his movement. When he finally reached Will he peered at the boy through the little rectangular glasses that were perched on his beak-like nose.

"How do, chipper?" the station master said in a friendly tone. "Be ye a Sheere-folk Vacky from middlin' Lunnon or praper Suth Seaxna from coast?"

"I think so," Will said. He hadn't understood a word the man had said except for the word 'coast'.

The station master's fingers reached for Will's evacuee label and lifted it close to his eyes.

"Ah, Mus Maskall, sureleye." He nodded. "He bain't here yetner, be he chipper? Tis unaccountable, howsumdever, he'll be anigh I rackon."

Will's head was spinning. Did everyone here speak as incomprehensibly as this station master? Will pointed hesitantly at the village to his left, the only visible sign of human habitation in this green expanse that seemed so overwhelmingly devoid of familiarity.

"That be Nickleby," the station master nodded. "Disyer be Nickleby station. We took the sign down all-along-of the war, to confuse Hun sodgers. Mus Maskall's farm be atween Nickleby and Wolfden, he'll have ta stride 'cross the Wyrde Woods."

The station master pointed northwards at the mass of woods and then left again, leaving Will to take a seat on the single platform bench next to the station master's post, feeling miserable and utterly alone. He took off his helmet and turned it in his hands. If Great Uncle Maskall spoke the same ubble-gubble the station master did then he felt sure his current sense of being stranded in the middle of nowhere might last a long time. It struck Will that not forgetting who he was might be a harder proposition than he had previously thought.

Will reminded himself that Gaffer held Great Uncle Maskall in high esteem. They had talked about him on the way back from the seafront to Gaffer's house on Ashton Street, after meeting Tommy Tickle.

"Have you ever met my Great Uncle Maskall?" Will had asked.

"Aye, I have," Gaffer had nodded. "Four times I've met him."

"What is he like?"

Gaffer had paused for a moment to catch his breath. It had been a steep climb from the Kingswood Flat.

"He reminded me of his own brother, though less impulsive perhaps, feet rooted firmly in the soil. Not as likely to act on his whims."

"My other grandfather?"

"Wilfred Maskall, a charming rogue," Gaffer's face had transformed into one of warm wonder and Will had been intrigued. "Wilfred and I served together."

Will and Gaffer had resumed walking and reached the beginning of Ashton Street.

"In the Great War?" Will's eyes had grown. Much as he always tried Gaffer was tight-lipped about his war experiences. On rare occasions a few words would escape from him, to be pounced upon by Will who was fascinated by the subject.

"Before the Great War, at the turn of the century," Gaffer had answered. "We were in the Sussex. In the 1st Battalion of the Royal Sussex Regiment, part of Brigadier Hamilton's 21st Brigade in South Africa. A fine leader of men, Hamilton was."

He had stopped talking for a moment, his eyes distant and Will had reckoned that memories were flashing by. The boy had kept his silence; it was the best way to encourage Gaffer to spill some more of his past once those memories started flowing.

"We fought side by side at Doornkop and Diamond Hill. Advancing on that hill, I were scared. The Boers had artillery on both flanks and their infantry was well-dug in on that hill. The Boers were a cunning foe, clever and lethally efficient. We couldn't even see where we were going on account of the dust kicked up by the bullets and smoke from the shells fired at us. All the while, Wilfred is loudly describing in detail the delights of a countryside picnic on a fine English summer's day. 'Lads', he said, 'don't forget to bring a Sussex Rose for they wilt if kept indoors and come to full bloom in the sunshine.' He kept the lot of us on our feet and moving forward without faltering or undue hurry."

Gaffer had chuckled.

"After that we fought at Meyer's Kop. And then Abraham's Kraal where Wilfred copped a bullet, as you know."

"I didn't know, Gaffer, you never told me," Will had protested.

Gaffer had given Will a sideways look. "Wilfred died in my arms, Will. A painful memory."

Will's mind had staggered with that information. Jamie had come to his mind and Will had realised that Gaffer probably understood his pain all too well.

"When I came back to England in '02 I visited his family, at Maskall Farm in the Weald. To tell them of his passing, twould be more personal than just the official notice they had received, or so I reckoned. Wilfred's younger brother Fred, your Great Uncle, appreciated my coming a great deal. That was when I first met George, your father, a toddler then."

Will's mind had continued to spin with all the new revelations.

"George never met his father. Fred Maskall raised him as his own alongside his own daughter Liz." They had been approaching Gaffer's house and Gaffer had suddenly sounded tired and eager to wrap up the story. "When Fred wrote me nigh on two decades later to say George had Wilfred's itch for adventure and wanted to see the wider world I welcomed George into this here house in Brighton. I was not going to let Wilfred's son sleep in the park or stay in a hostel, was I?"

They had stopped in front of the terraced house Gaffer owned. It was small. Gaffer's tailoring business took up all of the ground floor and Will, his mum and his grandparents lived in the two-roomed first floor. There was a kitchen of sorts in the basement where the cooking and laundry were done.

"Course, the first thing George did in Brighton was to fall head over heels for my daughter," Gaffer had sighed dramatically and Will had laughed at that. "Your great uncle came to Brighton for the wedding, and your Gran and I were invited to the farm for Christmas in the year before you were born, lad. In fact, I suspect you were conceived on that farm for those two were forever sneaking off into sheds and haylofts."

Gaffer had grinned, "Don't you ever tell your mum or Gran I said that."

Will had shook his head and grinned back.

"Then Fred and his Betty came down for George's funeral," Gaffer had said after which there had been a short awkward silence before the two had gone into the twitten which led to the back door that was used as the entrance to the residential part; the front door was for customers.

Will looked at a weed struggling to grow between the bricks of Nickleby Station's platform. It was odd to not be following in his father's footsteps but to reverse them. The one from Maskall Farm to Brighton. The other from Brighton to Maskall Farm.

"Doornkop, Diamond Hill," Will whispered. He had committed the names to memory. His grandfather Wilfred was a war hero, just like Gaffer was. "Meyer's Kop, Abraham's Kraal."

"All of them a middling stride from Sussex, sureleye." A deep voice interrupted Will.

Will looked up to see a tall man in the somewhat crudely made green uniform of the Home Guard standing astride the platform. He had sergeant's stripes on his sleeve, wore a Brodie helmet, and had a rifle slung over his shoulder. His face was unshaven, covered in grey stubble and his blue eyes shone brightly.

"By Geemeny," the man shook his head. "You're the spitting image of your gaffer and dad, so you are. Tis unaccountable."

"Great Uncle Maskall?" Will stood up.

"The very same," the man held out a great big hand and Will shook it firmly. "And as I pointed out you can be naun other than William Maskall."

Will nodded.

Not much later he found himself sitting on the box of a small wagon pulled by two sturdy draught horses, Great Uncle Maskall by his side. Will put on his own helmet.

"Is it far, Great Uncle Maskall?"

"It's anigh," his great uncle replied, leaving Will none the wiser. "Tis a mouthful, bain't it? The great uncle business? And it bain't fitting for you to call me Fred."

"Mister Maskall?" Will ventured.

"That won't do at all," Great Uncle Maskall shook his head. "Far too fancy for a simple farmer alike me."

Will thought about it for a while.

"Could I call you Gruncle?" He asked.

"Gruncle? I middling like that, so I do, and naun has ever called me so afore, it'll be a special name atween you and me."

"Very well, Gruncle," Will smiled.

"That looks like a fine tin hat you're wearing, sureleye," Gruncle Maskall said as the rooftops of Nickleby came closer.

"Mark 1, 1916," Will said proudly.

"A proper one, the bettermost. I didn't ken you were in Civil Defence in Brighton. Air Raid Precaution?"

Will shook his head sadly. "I was too young for the ARP, they said. And they laughed at me when I applied to join the LDV."

Gruncle Maskall steered the wagon onto a side road which turned right and bypassed Nickleby to their left. There was a timbered pub on the near corner and behind that the dark edge of trees which marked the boundary of the Wyrde Woods.

"This is the North Woods Lane, we're on," Gruncle Maskall explained. "It runs all the way to Mordrove, passing the village of Wolfden. Maskall Farm is a ways south of Wolfden."

Will nodded.

"We'll be coming back disyer way next week when I take you to the surgery in Odesby to have that head of yours looked at."

Will carefully placed a hand on the bandage around his head, nearly knocking his helmet off.

"It was a shrapnel wound," he said. "The doctor at the Royal Sussex County Hospital said I was lucky I had a thick skull."

Gruncle Maskall laughed heartily. "A fine Maskall trait!"

Will laughed too.

"A Sussex tradition too," Gruncle Maskall said and recited:

*And you may pook
and you may shove*

but a Sussex pig
he wun't be druv.

"Sussex wun't be druv!" Will exclaimed; it was a favourite saying of his.

"Sussex wun't be druv, indeed," Gruncle Maskall said. "And those of the Wyrde Woods the least of all. Tis an unfortunate circumstance of the war that you and I do naun see eye to eye and may well be equally stubborn."

"Did…? Was…?" Will was confused for a moment and worried that he had said something wrong to cause this disagreement his great uncle referred to.

"I suspect," Gruncle Maskall said with a small grin, "that you may be experiencing your arrival as an exile."

Will said nothing for the observation was a sharp one.

"Whereas, to my eyes, tis more of a homecoming. You have many roots in the Wyrde Woods, young Mus Maskall."

"Grandfather Wilfred," Will said.

"Aye, and your dad George and my Liz who grew up together as brother and sister afore he went to Brighton and she went to Lunnon. Many generations afore that as well, some time ago and longer. So twill be something of a contest, Will. Your perspective 'gainst mine. A battle of wills, if you will, Will."

Will grinned, "May the best man win."

Gruncle Maskall laughed at that.

They were silent for some time after that as dense woodlands rolled by on both sides of the North Woods Lane. It was not an awkward silence though, they were already comfortable in each other's company and Will thought that was a good thing. The woodlands to his right carried on and on, menacing and dark. The ones to his left were increasingly broken up by fields and small dirt roads which led to farms set a distance away from the North Woods Lane. At one such junction Gruncle Maskall clucked his horses to the left and the wagon rumbled onto the smaller road through a set of copses after which barren fields were revealed. These stretched to a small thatched farmhouse surrounded by outbuildings and orchards behind which meadows rolled up a gentle slope to meet the edge of a forest.

"Maskall Farm," Gruncle Maskall said with pride in his voice. "Your ancestral home, William Maskall, your kin have been scratching along here since the days of King Aelle, and you are welcome here."

"Thank you," Will said, not quite knowing how to respond. He craned his neck this way and that to take in the farm as they approached it.

"Has Eric told you about Maisy?" Gruncle Maskall asked.

"Huh, no, I've not hear anything about a Maisy, Gruncle."

"Liz's daughter, my granddaughter. Eleven years old, grew up in Lunnon and as bright as a magpie."

Will tried to draw a mental map of the family tree. His dad George and Gruncle's daughter Liz had been cousins, that would make Maisy…

"I don't hold much with the dunnamy times removed business," Gruncle Maskall was clearly pursuing the same train of thought. "Tis unaccountable, the two of you are cousins, Will, and that's that, sureleye."

Will nodded. He had never known he had a cousin and suddenly looked forward to meeting this Maisy one day.

"London, you said?" He asked Gruncle Maskall.

"Aye, howsumdever, a Vacky, just alike yourself."

"She's here?" The news pleased Will.

"Aye, and the two of you will be sharing George and Liz's old room. There's just the two bedrooms in the farmhouse."

"Oh," Will replied. He had never had a room of his own. Back in Brighton, Gaffer's living room was transformed into a bedroom each night as two thin hard matresses were brought in for Will and his mum. Perhaps Mum used both matresses now, he certainly hoped so, she would be more comfortable that way. To have an actual bedroom seemed like a luxury to Will; having to share it with a girl didn't greatly appeal to him though.

"I am sure the two of you will get along," Gruncle Maskall smiled as the wagon rumbled onto the farmyard and he brought the horses to a halt. The words didn't greatly reassure Will for something in Gruncle's tone told him it might not be all that easy.

"I'll be right back," Gruncle Maskall told his horses and guided Will to the door of the farmhouse. He opened it and ushered Will in. The boy found himself in a large kitchen, dominated by a central table and a great number of facilities which shamed the meagre excuse for a kitchen in Gaffer's basement; a great iron cooking range, a sink and water pump, another fire place, cupboards and shelves. A woman stood at the sink, broad and with long silver hair. She turned around and Will saw that she had a kind open face.

"My goodness!" She exclaimed.

"I felt much the same, Betty," Gruncle Maskall greeted her. "This is William Maskall."

"Hullo, Great Aunt Maskall," Will said shyly.

"Oh my goodness," his great aunt repeated and wiped her hands on her apron. "'Tis like George walked into the kitchen after dunnamy years." She shook her head. "You're welcome here Will, more than welcome. But naun of this 'great aunt' business if you please, Gran or Granny will do."

Will nodded. He already had a Gran so he opted for Granny.

"You'll be wanting a cup of tea and a nibble, naun doubt? Growing lads are always hungry, I recollect. Walking stomachs. Some bread and homemade jam? Do sit down, lad."

Will smiled at her. "That would be wonderful, Granny Maskall."

"I'll see to the horses," Gruncle Maskall pulled the door open again. "And I'll bring in your luggage afterwards, Will."

"Thank you Gruncle Maskall," Will said and walked to the table where he pulled up a chair. As he sat down he felt the day's long journey had finally come to an end.

4. A Hopeful Ride

Eddie cheered up the moment he perceived they were going to ride on a farm wagon drawn by a team of three horses which were hitched in a single file. Mr Hornsby lifted the children's luggage onto the wagon's bed and then helped them up the box. Joining them he flicked the reigns and clucked. The horses obediently moved forwards as one and the wagon jolted into motion.

"You were very brave back there, lass," Mr Hornsby said to Brenda as the wagon rolled north out of Odesby.

"I promised Mum," Brenda bit her lip. She already missed Mum terribly, and Dad too.

"And you kept your promise," Mr Hornsby said. "I am sure the Pattersons will honour it."

"What if they don't?"Brenda asked softly.

"I am sure they will, lass," Mr Hornsby waved away her fear. "They seem nice, a mite peculiar perhaps."

"Peculiar?" Brenda's eyes grew wide

"Oh, don't you mind me," Mr Hornsby laughed. "I'm just a simple farmer and anything a stride from the Wyrde Woods is peculiar in my eyes, sureleye."

"The Wyrde Woods?" Brenda asked. She wished she could stay with Mr Hornsby instead. He had mentioned that he had children and seemed nice. She didn't think much of the name of the woods though, it seemed rather silly.

"A name for the whole area north of Odesby, howsumdever, properly speaking, the woodlands yonder." Mr Hornsby pointed to their left where woodlands rose and fell as far as the eye could see.

"Farm?" Eddie asked, finally taking his eyes off the horses.

"That's right, lad," Mr Hornsby confirmed. "The Hornsby Farm. Been in my family since the wizard Merlin's days."

There was a pride in his voice which made Brenda smile.

"Wizard," Eddie nodded solemnly and stared at Mr Hornsby with wide eyes.

"There's me what lives in the farmhouse," Mr Hornsby continued. "With the bettermost woman in Sussex."

"Your wife?" Brenda guessed.

"Indeed, so she is," Mr Hornsby nodded and then clucked his horses to the side of the road to let a small convoy of army lorries pass.

"Jenny Hornsby will be wanting to meet you, I am sure Brenda, I reckon the two of you will get on fine."

"It would be lovely to meet your wife," Brenda said, eager to meet Mrs Hornsby for she sounded like a kind person already.

"Along with my three chavvies, my brother Jasper and his three chavvies."

Six children at the farm! It sounded like fun and Brenda longed to reach their destination.

"Jasper's eldest, Lizzie, is your age," Mr Hornsby continued. "I suspect she'll want to meet you too." He clucked the horses into faster motion and steered them back onto the road.

Brenda smiled.

"So you're welcome to call at the farm house, is what I have been meaning to say," Mr Hornsby said.

"The people who…" Brenda paused. *The people who sent you to fetch a child from the market.* She could hardly say that though.

"Mister and Missus Patterson live in the old cottage. What used to be the Hornsby Farm dunnamy centuries ago. We were ordered to fix it up, to house refugees. There's a big kitchen, a large bedroom and a small bedroom, aside the barn and outbuildings."

Mr Hornsby steered the wagon off the road, onto a side road to their left. It was much more narrow and dipped in and out of sight, often screened by the great tall hedges which bordered the fields. There were two huddles of rooftops and trees to be seen, the nearest about halfway up the road. The outer edge of the fields around these sets of buildings was made up by the edge of the Wyrde Woods.

Mr Hornsby looked at Eddie and smiled. "I've hung up a swing too, lad. In the old cottage orchard. Do you like to go on swings?"

Eddie nodded and held out his bag of sweets. "Do you like a sweet?"

"Would you like a sweet, Eddie." Brenda corrected him.

"That's what I said," Eddie frowned at her.

"Don't mind if I do," Mr Hornsby laughed and fished a gobstopper our of the bag. "I've got a sweet tooth. Thank you, lad. Mighty kind of you. Though I'll save it for later. You're both welcome at Hornsby Farm, Brenda and Edward of Brighton."

Eddie beamed so heartily that he made Brenda laugh. Perhaps a little too loud but there was a lot of relief which needed to come out. Though Mr Hornsby looked alarmingly rough and rugged he was really a most friendly and funny man. Brenda felt comfortable in his presence and wished again that she and Eddie could stay with his large family instead. Just fanciful thinking, she berated herself. At any rate, he had made clear she was welcome to visit and she felt much more relaxed about her strange uprooted situation because of that.

Mr Hornsby stopped the horses outside the first set of buildings. There was a small grey cottage; its walls made from crudely shaped stones of all sizes and slate tiles on the roof. Opposite the cottage, across thirty feet of yard, stood a barn. It had the same circumference as the cottage but had two stories, opposed to the cottage's single one. The far end of the yard was faced by a row of sheds and stables.

Mr Hornsby helped Brenda and Eddie off the box; picking them up and gently setting them down.

"We'll go say hullo first," Mr Hornsby decided. "And then I'll fetch your luggage from the wagon."

Followed by Brenda and Eddie he walked across the yard to the door which was set centrally. There were two small latticed windows, one on each corner of the cottage.

Mr Hornsby stopped by the door and knocked on it.

He smiled at Brenda and Eddie, probably to encourage them because they were trying to make themselves as small as possible.

The door opened and a sour-faced woman dressed in an old fashioned black dress with long sleeves and a high neck peered out.

Eddie's lip trembled as he looked at the woman and Brenda understood why; the woman looked a little bit scary, not friendly at all.

"Yes, Mr Hornsby?" She asked in a sharp voice.

"The Vackies you were assigned, Missus Patterson." Mr Hornsby smiled broadly and indicated the children. "Brenda and Edward from Brighton."

"I only agreed to the one," the woman frowned. "Please take the boy back."

Eddie whimpered and seized Brenda's hand. She gave it a reassuring squeeze even though she felt her own spirits sinking fast.

"Two for the price of one today, I reckon you've got a bargain," Mr Hornsby continued smiling, though Brenda noticed that his eyes no longer twinkled. "Though you are welcome, of course, Missus Patterson, to discuss the terms of your stay here with the local billeting officer."

"No, that won't be necessary," Mrs Patterson said quickly.

"I'll fetch their luggage then," Mr Hornsby started walking back to the wagon.

Mrs Patterson looked Brenda and Eddie up and down, radiating disapproval.

"Well, you'd best come in then," she said at last and disappeared into the cottage.

5. The Invisible Cousin

Gruncle Maskall led Will up a narrow pair of stairs. There was a small landing there with doors on either side and one at the end.

"Two bedrooms up here, the stairs to the loft behind the third," Gruncle Maskall explained when Will had caught up with him on the landing. "Outhouse at the back of the house and a tin bathtub in the kitchen for the Saturday bath."

Will nodded. To him the small farmhouse seemed spacious.

"And here we are…" Gruncle Maskall smiled and swung open one of the side doors. Will stepped in, uncertain as to what to expect. The room seemed small at first. The blackout curtains had been drawn back and two latticed windows let light through which fell on the single bed which stood there, the frame a sturdy wood construction topped by a thick mattress. Next to the bed was a crate with small two shelves built into it. There was a closet at the foot of the bed. Will could see that it was empty for the doors stood open.

"That used to be your father's bed," Gruncle Maskall said.

"Really?" Will liked that idea, he quite liked all the space too, it seemed very homely. He recalled that he was supposed to be sharing the room with his cousin just as his eyes noted that the room was actually much larger, but somebody had run lengths of rope along the ceiling from which hung a wall of blankets. The makeshift wall ended on the floor and started about twenty inches below the ceiling. To judge by the light-fall in there, the two windows he could see on his side of the room had twins on the other side of the woollen barrier.

"Are you still barricaded in, Maisy-mine?" Gruncle Maskall called out.

There was a snort and then a muffled grunt from the other side of the blankets.

"Your cousin Will has arrived. Don't you want to say 'hullo'?" Gruncle Maskall continued. "'Tis polite, you know?"

"Erm, hullo," Will addressed the blankets. "I'm Will."

"WE SHALL NEVER SURRENDER!" The blanket fort hollered defiantly.

Gruncle Maskall looked at Will and shrugged. "Maisy needs some time to adjust, that's all."

The invisible cousin behind the blankets snorted again and then fell silent as Gruncle Maskall helped Will unpack his suitcase and bags and place Will's few possessions in the closet and improvised bed side table.

"Well, that's done," Gruncle Maskall said when they were finished. "Your gammer will have tea ready soon. She'll ring the bell outside the door, to let all know it's done. Saves her tramping around the farmyard looking for me."

He turned to the curtain. "You may want to consider your surrender at teatime, lass."

"No surrender! I'd rather be eaten by boggerts, ain't it?" The blanket fort answered with stubborn conviction.

Will's grand uncle shrugged again and then winked at Will. "Have it your way, I admire your resolution, Captain Robbins."

The blanket fort stayed silent and Gruncle Maskall left the room to go back downstairs. Will decided to ignore his new-found cousin behind her curtain. Instead, he settled on the bed and smiled when he understood just how soft and comfortable the mattress was. He lay down to test the big pillows and his smile grew when his head sank into fluffy softness. At least he would sleep just fine in this strange new world; he had never had such a luxurious bed to sleep in. Maybe he would just sleep until the war was over and he could go back to Brighton.

Will was wondering just how long it would be possible to sleep and how best to test this when he noted a small movement from the corner of his eye. The curtains had shifted a little bit, as if someone had created a narrow gap to peek through. Will hoped it was a first crack in his cousin's armour as he was getting most curious about Maisy. So far, at least, she wasn't like any of the girls he had studiously ignored at school when he still believed all girls were silly. Dorothy and Brenda, the two Brighton girls he knew a little, had already taught him some were only moderately silly and maybe this cousin would be like them. She could build good blanket forts at any rate and that was a plus.

Will sat up on the bed and thought he saw another tiny shiver in the folds where two blanket ends met.

"If you think," the invisible cousin spoke in a low dramatic tone, "to come anywhere near my side of the room, or even blooming look at it, I will cut your skull open with a rusty hacksaw, cross me heart and hope to die."

Will rubbed the bandage over the part of his scalp which had been rent open by shrapnel.

"The Jerries already tried that," Will joked, as he solemnly vowed to stay well away from his cousin's side of the room.

"Did they?" There was melodious curiosity in the voice but then it fell back into the ominous threatening one which reminded him of the voiceovers at the pictures. "And I will scoop your brains out with a blunt teaspoon, ain't it? Feed them to the pigs, so I will."

"I'll stay away from your side of the room," Will grimaced. "A BLUNT teaspoon? Seriously?"

The bell rang outside. It was teatime and Will realised he was famished after the day's long journey even after just having eaten Granny's sandwiches. He jumped up.

"Are you coming down for tea?" He asked but there was no answer, so he went downstairs by himself.

§ § § § § § §

"Your gaffer and I," Gruncle Maskall explained to Will as they sat down at the kitchen table. "Had exchanged a few letters as to the notion of you staying here. The last I heard of it, howsumdever, it weren't to your mum's liking."

"Next thing," Granny Maskall picked up the story as she served the food. "Postman brings us a telegram to let us know you were on your way."

"I am sorry," Will said automatically as his eyes drank in the sight of all the food on his plate. There were roast potatoes, golden and crispy, as well as fresh green beans, onion gravy and what looked suspiciously like a pork chop. "Is that real meat?"

"It's not much," Granny Maskall apologized. "All-along-of the rationing, sureleye."

"Not much?" Will exclaimed. "It's fit for a king!"

Granny Maskall beamed.

"You'll find rationing is bettermost on a farm, Will." Gruncle Maskall's eyes twinkled. "I suspect there is less fresh food in Brighton?"

Will shrugged uncomfortably. He didn't know for sure if there were shortages. He just knew that food prices had risen considerably since the war had started and his family wasn't well off. They couldn't afford a great deal; certainly not many fresh products and he had only ever eaten pork chops once when he had been invited over to the Hall's home on Sussex Street in celebration of Jamie's twelfth birthday.

Will's face fell at the memory. Jamie wouldn't be having any more birthdays.

"If that lass bain't down soon," Granny Maskall tutted. "I'll go upstairs to fetch her, drag her down by the ear if I must."

"Maisy's got a healthy appetite," Gruncle Maskall said. "It will drive her down soon enow. I'm naun waiting for the food to get cold though."

He nodded at Will and tucked in. Will eagerly speared one of the potatoes on his fork, his belly rumbling happy appreciation.

"Your gaffer wrote about what happened, Will," Granny Maskall said as she cut into her pork chop. "So we understand the urgency, though truth be told, George's son would be welcome here no matter what the circumstances, sureleye."

Will nodded as he debated cutting into his pork chop too. It looked succulent but he decided to save it for last and attacked his green beans instead.

"Howsumdever," Gruncle Maskall said between two mouthfuls, "Maisy only heard this morning, just alike us and was a mite tessy, having grown attached to the notion of having a room of her own, I reckon. Tis unaccountable, I've been having to share my room for decades with this middling woman here."

Will grinned at that but then frowned. "But if it is her room…"

"Oakum!" Granny Maskall shook her head. "Maisy is a Vacky, just alike yourself. Twere Liz and George's room afore that, and they shared it for years. Her mum and your dad. Best of friends they were. Maisy is a dear but like as not to stir up a fuss every now and then, she's fond of causing a scamble, she is. Takes after her middling gaffer, I reckon."

"Keep in mind," Gruncle Maskall added, "that we'd like for you to get along, howsumdever, to my mind it's best to let the two of you sort that out atween yourselves."

Will nodded, that would probably work better. His mind was mostly on George Maskall anyways. Mum had never spoken of his dad much apart from saying he had been a good man. It was odd and fascinating to hear so many references to his father here. He would sleep in his dad's bed tonight. His unknown father had grown up here, familiar with all the things that seemed so new and strange to Will.

Will looked around the large farm kitchen again, seeing it through this different light. The kitchen had an uneven brick floor and sturdy ancient beams on the ceiling. A large chimney area was fronted by a kitchen range which had enough iron to build a small locomotive, Will reckoned. There was another open fire place with saucepans and kettles suspended from hooks, as well as hams which had presumably been hung there to be smoked. The old stone sink had a pump beside it so that water could be drawn inside the house. Various doorways led to the farmyard, two sculleries and a small hallway which divided the kitchen from the much smaller front room and contained the staircase as well. His dad would have walked over the kitchen's brick floor a hundred thousand times and considered the farm kitchen as familiar as Will did Gaffer's house in Brighton. It was strange and at the same time a little thrilling because it made Will feel closer to his father.

Maisy didn't come down and Granny Maskall put her plate aside when it was time to do the washing up. Afterwards they had a cup of tea and listened to the war news on the wireless in the front room, which was formal and neat, very different from the busy energy Will had sensed in the kitchen. The main news was that the aerial bombardments of London continued in all intensity but that the autumn weather had started in earnest, postponing the expected German invasion until the spring. Will sighed a breath of relief for Brighton.

"I'm worried about Maisy, Fred." Granny Maskall said when the wireless switched to music. "She only had half her breakfast this morning afore she became tessy. What if she needs to go to the outhouse?"

"I heard her scurrying up and down the middling rain pipe earlier," Gruncle Maskall said. "So that's been taken care of, sureleye."

Will frowned at that; his mind's eye had envisaged this Maisy to be large and duly intimidating. Now it sounded like she was agile and strong as well.

"She must be famished," Granny Maskall shook her head.

"'Tis bad enough we allow her these Lunnon dramatics," Gruncle Maskall said. "I told her she'd be welcome for tea if she came downstairs. I can hardly take food up to her after that, can I?"

"Maybe if…" Will said and then shut up. Though Gruncle Maskall and Granny Maskall seemed very nice people he hardly knew them well enough to start making household proposals. It was generally not something children were expected to do anyway.

"Maybe what?" Gruncle Maskall asked. "Spit it out lad."

"Well," Will looked from one to the other. "What if I were to take it upstairs without your permission?"

"Steal food from us, on your first day here?" Gruncle Maskall asked sternly.

Will shrugged helplessly, it was the best idea he could come up with and he wanted to be useful. He also thought it was a good way of signalling his good intentions to somebody who was obviously displeased with his arrival. To his surprise Granny Maskall started to chuckle and then Gruncle Maskall guffawed.

"I think that might just do the trick, sureleye. Your gaffer was right when he wrote you were deedy," he said. "You'll be saving us worry, you won't be kept awake by Maisy's rumbling tummy tonight, and nobody needs to surrender. Go on lad, carry out your thievery."

Will smiled.

§ § § § § § §

Will entered the room carrying the plate Granny Maskall had set aside for Maisy. Even though the food was cold now and the gravy had started to congeal, it still looked temptingly delicious.

"Maisy," Will called out in a low conspiratorial tone.

"I got me hacksaw ready, ain't it?" Maisy replied behind her curtain. "And me axe. It's dead sharp, cleave right through your belly it will, and your guts will be trailing out. I'll try not to trip over them cause I'm a nice person, ain't I?"

"I brought you food," Will replied. "I am putting the plate down here."

Will put down the plate at the bottom of the blanket-curtain and tapped the floorboards to indicate the location. There was a long silence before Maisy asked: "Did Gran or Gramps tell you to take it up?"

"No," Will replied. "I took it without asking."

He had not really asked, not directly anyway, so technically he wasn't telling a fib.

"Gran will skin you alive," Maisy said with evident satisfaction in her voice. "She does you know. She skins me almost every week. Pure torture. You'd best try to escape tonight. Get as far away as you can, ain't it? I'll try and create a distraction if you want. Run and live. Or stay and die."

Will raised an eyebrow at that and watched a surprisingly small hand appear next to the plate, locate it, and pull it towards the curtain where a low plate-sized gap had appeared.

Will grinned as he changed into his pajamas and heard his cousin noisily devour her food. A healthy appetite indeed, but he himself would have been faint with hunger this long after teatime.

He got into bed, relishing the mattress again, as well as the weight of the woollen blankets which promised warmth on chilly nights.

"Good night, Maisy," he said. There was no answer and Will felt a brief flash of disappointment. He consoled himself by concluding that he had tried his best at any rate. After that he was briefly worried that he would wake to find his mysterious cousin lumbering over him deep in the night, ready to saw his limbs off with her rusty hacksaw but sleep rapidly diminished these fears. Will was halfway to dreamland when he heard a very soft: "Good night, Will."

6. The Pattersons

Brenda stepped into the cottage. Eddie clutched her hand tightly and pressed Buntings to his face, clearly unhappy. Mrs Patterson waited in a small hallway. She pointed to Brenda's left.

"That's the master bedroom, this door here," Mrs Patterson pointed at the door opposite the front door, "leads to your bedroom and this one leads to the kitchen, there is no front room which is one of the many rural curiosities we've had to put up with. It's all dreadfully primitive, like that horrible outhouse we have to use."

Brenda followed Mrs Patterson into the kitchen. A man sat at the kitchen table in the centre of the room and Brenda looked around quickly, taking in the elaborate kitchen range and other facilities which seemed adequate enough to her. The cottage wasn't all that much smaller than her home in Brighton and she couldn't understand what was primitive about it. Perhaps the outhouse. Mrs Patterson had specifically mentioned that. Brenda knew that posh houses had indoor ones, unlike the street where she lived, they all had outhouses there.

"What's this?" The man looked at the children with irritation. He was balding with wild wings of silver hair on the sides of his head and wore little round glasses on his pointy nose.

"The mandatory evacuees," Mrs Patterson told him. "This is Mr Patterson, children."

"I am pleased to meet you, Mr Patterson," Brenda said. "I'm Brenda." She turned to Eddie. "Say hello, Edward."

"Please to meet, I am Edward," Eddie mumbled into Buntings.

"I was only expecting the one," Mr Patterson grumbled.

"It has been made clear to me, in a rustic manner, that there was no choice in the matter," Mrs Patterson replied.

"We'll see about that," Mr Patterson said, "I'll ask Hornsby to take the boy back to Odesby tomorrow."

"With Brenda?" Eddie asked.

"Shush, Edward," Brenda said and hoped that Mr Hornsby would come in soon.

"Actually," Mr Patterson said, pausing as he peered at the children over his glasses. "What is the government remuneration for evacuees?"

"For the Vacky chavvies?" Mr Hornsby came into the kitchen with the children's luggage. "Ten shillings sixpence a week for the first child, and eight shillings sixpence for the second, Mister Patterson."

"Really?" Mr Patterson smiled for the first time.

"Please take the children's luggage into the small bedroom," Mrs Patterson said to Mr Hornsby. "It's the first door on the…"

"Beggin your pardon, Missus Patterson, but I know my way around the cottage," Mr Hornsby said and winked at Brenda as he picked up all the luggage again.

"I'll open the doors for you, Mr Hornsby," Brenda said quickly. "If I may?" She looked at Mrs Patterson who nodded. "Come on Eddie."

The two children escaped into the hallway with Mr Hornsby and Brenda opened the bedroom door. There was a small unmade bed to one side and a rickety closet and narrow table and chair on the other. Best of all, there was a window through which Brenda could see the orchard and the swing Mr Hornsby had talked about.

"Naun much space," Mr Hornsby set the luggage on the bed. "You'll have to share the bed."

"Oh, Eddie is very small," Brenda said. She even thought it would be nice to be close to him at night and she knew for sure that Eddie would draw comfort from the fact.

Mr Hornsby peered into the closet, there were some folded bedclothes there; sheets and blankets.

"Very well, lass," Mr Hornsby said and walked out of the room again.

Brenda heard him stick his head through the kitchen door and say: "I'll be off now, good evening Mister Patterson, good evening Missus Patterson."

"Yes, thank you," Mrs Patterson replied. "Please close the door behind you."

Mr Hornsby closed the kitchen door, shaking his head. He looked into the small room.

"Take care, Brenda, goodbye Eddie."

Eddie smiled and waved.

"Goodbye Mr Hornsby, thank you for everything," Brenda gave him her best smile.

He grinned and gave her another wink and then he was gone. Brenda sat down on the bed, unsure as what she should do.

"Tigger?" Eddie suggested hopefully.

Brenda nodded. "Why not? Reading a Pooh story will make it just like home. I suppose we should unpack our things first though."

She proceeded to do just that, putting the small piles of neatly folded clothes into the cupboard and dividing the table between the few personal items they had been able to bring, as well as a hairbrush, comb, toothbrushes and toothpaste. Then she made the bed with the bedding she had taken out of the closet. The blankets looked threadbare and thin and she hoped they wouldn't get too cold.

When Brenda was done she and Eddie sat down on the bed and she read him from *The House at Pooh Corner*, Eddie's favourite book. Her little brother leant against her contentedly, still clutching Buntings. When Brenda turned the page she smiled at Margaret Elizabeth, whom she had arranged centre-stage on the table, with Will's Brighton pebbles in front of the doll, and for a short sweet moment it did almost seem like they were home.

7. Brave New World

When Will woke up late the next morning his cousin Maisy had already left for school. Granny Maskall explained to Will that he had to have a week's more rest before they would take him to a surgery in nearby Odesby for a final check-up. Until then Will wouldn't be required to attend school. This suited him fine, he was a little nervous about starting at a brand new school where he didn't know anybody. He was also interested in visiting Odesby, because that place, he knew, was where Brenda and Eddie would have got off the train which carried them all out of Brighton.

Gruncle Maskall was out and about on farm business and Granny Maskall served Will a sumptuous breakfast which included a rasher of bacon and an egg; though she told him - with a wink - to keep that egg a secret. It was meant for the war effort, but Granny Maskall was a firm believer in the beneficial health effects of home cooking and told Will she intended to spoil him as long as he had his bandage on. Will agreed with her wholeheartedly as he cut his bacon and egg into tiny bites to make them last as long as possible. Back home they made do with powdered eggs most of the time and bacon was a rare luxury.

He spent the morning exploring the farm, wandering in and out of various barns and sheds. The farmyard would have made a brilliant setting for a

Western scenario to be played out but Will had no one to play with.

He decided to go for a walk. The Maskalls had mentioned the Wyrde Woods a few times and Will had gathered that they were on the opposite side of the main road so he decided that would be a good place to start exploring his new surroundings. Granny Maskall was quite insistent that Will shouldn't exert himself too much when he asked if he could walk to North Woods Lane and explore, but after he promised to be back shortly and be extra careful she relented.

Will equipped himself properly: helmet, gasmask, Spitfire, catapult, and ammo bag. He took his Class A Ammo marbles, for the Class B Ammo, the pebbles which he had picked up from the shingle beach near Banjo Groyne, were valuable to him now. He had stored them underneath his pillow and had woken up to discover the leather pouch clasped firmly in one of his hands.

Will found his way to the main road easily enough and there was a well-trodden footpath leading into the woods directly opposite to the Maskall Farm access road. The Wyrde Woods were a paradox to him. Whenever the Maskalls mentioned the name there was a certain reverence in their tone which led him to expect something extraordinary. Now that Will was in the Wyrde Woods he concluded that it seemed like an ordinary woods. Except, of course, at the same time it wasn't at all ordinary. His frame of reference for a wood was Queen's Park and Preston Park or the shaded country lanes just outside of Brighton but this was entirely different. There were no rooftops to be seen for one, nor traffic to be heard. There was some chitter from birds in the trees but other than that a serene silence reigned supreme and the sheer mass of trees was astonishing to Will, who had never seen so many together before.

Will stopped when he saw a small grassy clearing to his left and especially the three tall horse chestnuts which took center stage. He walked up to the trees with a smile on his face. Will and Jamie had known where to find every horse chestnut in the parks, squares, and churchyards of Brighton. They had checked them regularly in the autumn because you needed to be on the spot fast to collect the best conkers when the prickly fruit cases started dropping. His smile turned into a grin when he saw these trees were laden with fruit just short of ripening. The best conkers were matured in a dry place for a year of course, but he was certain he would find some prime samples here for immediate use. He hatched a plan to find loads more good specimens to dry out at the bottom of his closet. He was certain he would be back in Brighton before too long and how grand it would be to come back with a bag load of Class-A conkers and astonish the lads in Queen's Park with their poor town conkers. Last year he and Jamie had almost come out on top as Conker Kings of Queen's Park, after doing very well in Albion Hill too. He would miss this year's season but, oh just wait till next year! He made a mental note to visit the clearing at least twice a week from now on and then continued on his way.

Will had already heard passing aircraft several times that day so he didn't pay the far off hum much attention at first. It was easier to judge their distance in the countryside; devoid as it was of all the noises which pervaded a busy town so the planes could be heard coming from much further away. Moreover, he had yet to hear a single air raid warning, something which pleased him. In Brighton there had been days when they seemed to go off continuously and their echoes still hanted him.

Will came to the top of a low ridge from where the path led down into a series of valleys where the trees were less densely packed. He followed the path to the bottom of the first valley and when he got there the plane's engines sounded much closer. Will stopped and looked up; scanning the sky. He saw nothing but the steady hum continued to increase in volume; something was flying low and coming closer. Will shivered and edged to the side of the path where a big oak seemed to offer some shelter.

The growl became a roar when the familiar silhouette of a Junkers Ju88 appeared above the trees of the ridge and dipped slightly as it followed the contours of the ground below it. It seemed to be coming straight for Will and the boy froze like a startled rabbit transfixed by the sight of a predator swooping in for a kill. Will half expected bursts of machine gun fire and kept his eyes firmly locked on the closed bomb bay doors. *Don't let them open.* He had seen them open once, from a close distance, at school in Brighton. They had barely escaped a direct hit.

The Junkers sped towards him and Will started trembling violently, still frozen to the spot, paralyzed by fear. When the plane roared overhead Will felt an angry tear roll down his cheek and he grimaced with the pain of humiliation.

"BASTARDS" He shouted at the Junkers furiously, his voice suddenly jumping into a high pitch at the end of the expletive. He raised his hand to shake his fist at the Jerry plane but it held the Spitfire, so instead Will ran after the aircraft, keeping the toy high up in the air with its nose pointed at the Junkers. The German plane was fast gaining headway on him but Will ran for all he was worth, roaring at the top of his voice as his toy Spitfire pursued the Luftwaffe bomber.

"RATTATATAT!! RATTATAT! TAKE THAT YOU BLEEDING BASTARD!"

Blind fury possessed Will and he was so intent on shooting down the German plane that he barely registered a girl of his own age in a white dress by the side of the path, or the pig that accompanied her, an oddity which would ordinarily not have escaped his notice. Instead, he simply stampeded by, his vision clouded with a red rage.

It was almost as if the fading sound of the Junkers mocked Will; making fun of his initial cowardice and subsequent foolish attempt to chase it. He smarted with the agony of it and then stumbled over a root and went sprawling on the ground; the Spitfire flying out of his hand and landing onto the ground in front of him with an audible crack.

Will lifted his head and spat out a mouthful of dirt. He whimpered when he saw that the Spitfire's right wing had broken off. The Spitfire which Mr. Hall had so carefully crafted for Jamie, after which the two of them had spent hours painting the toy. Mr Hall had been brilliant in those father-son activities – often involving Will in them too. The last time he had seen Mr Hall was when Jamie's dad had been made...incomplete...by a German bomb. The same one that killed Jamie and wounded Will. Will had been covered in Mr Hall's blood and he had seen Jamie's corpse in the hospital. Gone. And now the Spitfire was gone too. Something snapped in Will; his eyes filled with tears and he crawled forwards to retrieve the plane and broken wing. He sat up, pressed the pieces to his chest and was racked by violent sobs.

§ § § § § § §

Will stumbled out of the Wyrde Woods feeling nauseous and disorientated; a chasm of desolate emptiness inside.

"Oi! You're not supposed to go walking in the Wyrde Woods on your own."

Will shook his head and forced his eyes to focus. Just a few yards from his position at the edge of the broad dirt road stood a young child, six, maybe seven.

She was wearing a rudimentary school uniform and had a book satchel and cardboard gasmask container swinging from her shoulder. Her hair was long and dark and there was an impish grin on her face.

Will vaguely recollected the blurry image of the girl in the white he had run past in the woods.

"I wasn't on my own," he answered lamely. "There was a girl in the woods."

"Chasing girls in the wood," the girl tutted. "Are you some kind of a bleeding pervert?"

"I wasn't…" Will felt confused. He didn't think he was a pervert, even though he had been keen on some of Brighton's saucier mutoscopes on the piers, and the bare legs of Dorothy, the girl he had shared a ward with at the Royal Sussex County Hospital. It wasn't any business of this stranger anyway. Since when did seven-year olds speak like this and grin so knowingly as this child was doing?

"None of your business, is it?" Will said.

"Not my business?" The child sounded outraged and waved her free arm dramatically. "I am condemned to share *MY* room with a bloody pervert and you tell me it ain't none of my business?"

Will stared at her. At long last he uttered a nonplussed "Maisy?"

"Who did you think I were?" Maisy asked. "Tarzan of the Apes?"

"No," Will shook his head but that made him dizzy so he stopped. "I was told you were eleven."

Maisy's eyes narrowed and she frowned. "And what makes you think I ain't?"

She placed her hands on her hips and straightened her back and broadened her shoulders and looked at him defiantly. It could have been funny but she carried the challenge off convincingly.

"You're a bit…" Will hesitated.

"A bit what?" Maisy asked. "Spit it out."

"Short," Will said.

Maisy's eyes grew wide and she threw a hand over her mouth in outraged shock and horror. Then her face contorted into a sneer.

"Cor, I ain't never heard that one before, have I?" She snorted derisively. "You've hurt my feelings now and I'll have to tell Gramps that you are a pervert, don't I?"

"You tell on people?" Will temporarily gained some of his old spirit back and his face managed to convey the utter disgust he felt for children who went blabbing to grown-ups.

"Of course I don't. I ain't a chaunt, am I?" Maisy said indignantly, before immediately contradicting herself. "He'll probably lock you up in the coal shed. I am his granddaughter, aren't I? He don't permit perverts near me you know. It'll be the coalshed for you every night. He might chop your bits off, I almost feel sorry for you. You're best off legging it to Nickleby station and catching a train back to Brighton. The station is that way."

Maisy smiled sweetly at the end of her torrent of words and pointed south along the North Woods Lane.

Will ignored Maisy's advice and began to cross the dirt road towards the entrance of the narrow road that led to Maskall Farm. Maisy fell into step next to him.

"That toy you're clutching," Maisy told Will. "It's broken. Just rubbish, ain't it?"

Something snapped in Will. The loss of Jamie's Spitfire was hard enough to bear without this hostile cousin rubbing salt in the wound.

"It ain't rubbish," he growled angrily.

"They need two wings to fly, Brighton-Boy. One wing ain't no good, is it? Only glocky nickeys would fly in a one-winged aeroplane. We learn these things in London, don't we? Greatest city in the world, London is. Have you ever been there?"

"No, and I don't want to go either," Will answered grumpily. Maisy was changing channels too frequently for his befuddled mind; ranging from friendly and amiable, to epically bombastic, to openly antagonistic, and back in the space of seconds.

"Cor blimey, but you ain't half miserable, are you?" Maisy shook her head. "No fun at all. We'll have to trade you in for some other cousin the way things are going. I'll arrange it at once."

"Just leave me alone," Will snapped. "Go away and leave me alone."

Maisy looked surprised and then for a fraction of a second she looked hurt as well and Will felt guilty about his outburst. His cousin's face hardened.

"Fine, have it your way," she declared and increased her pace, pulling ahead of Will with her head held high.

There was no sight of her when Will reached the farmyard. There were plenty of sounds though for Will could hear geese squawking in outrage and dogs barking in one of the outbuildings. He walked on with his head held down in dejection. It was not until he reached the middle of the yard that he noticed the gaggle of geese waggling towards him from the gateway which opened to the orchard and vegetable patch at the side of the farmhouse. The geese had their necks stretched out low and their wings spread out and regarded Will with fierce beady eyes. Alarmed, he backed up. As if encouraged the front goose, the largest of the lot, sped forward, hissing fury at Will.

"ENOW!" Gruncle Maskell's voice bellowed from the door opening of one of the low pig pens. He was wearing a farmers smock – a long old fashioned tunic – and came striding out with two lurchers at his heel. The geese beat a noisy and indignant retreat.

The lurchers approached Will, wagging their tails and thrusting their wet snouts at Will's free hand; he was still clutching the wrecked Spitfire to his chest with the other.

"Hugin and Munin," Gruncle Maskall said to Will. "My faithful companions and…Will, are you alright, lad?"

"I feel a bit fain't," Will admitted.

"You look as pale as a shim, lad. Let me take you inside."

Granny was in the kitchen and there was immediate concern on her face when Gruncle Maskall brought Will inside.

"Feeling a mite squimbly, are you Will? Come, sit down by the fire."

Will let himself be led to the fire where Granny wrapped a blanket around his shoulders.

Maisy came wandering in from the hallway and took in the scene.

"Blimey, Gran, I wouldn't mind getting a royal treatment when I came home from school, ain't it?"

"Hush Maisy, Will bain't feeling very well," Gruncle Maskall growled.

"Is that it?" Maisy asked. "There was me thinking he was always this cheerful."

"*Enow*, Maisy," Granny Maskall said and Will's cousin pouted.

"What happened, lad?" Gruncle Maskall asked.

Without a word Will held up the two parts of his broken Spitfire.

"It was Jamie's," he explained. To his embarassment he felt his eyes go moist and he blinked hard.

"I told him it were rubbish, no good broken, is it?" Maisy said.

"I've a mind to send you back into your barricade, lass," Gruncle Maskall said. "Will has been badly injured during a Jerry bombardment and his best friend was killed."

Will closed his eyes. To his surprise there was no witty retort from his cousin. He opened his eyes again and saw her fidgeting, looking at the floor with close interest, and then opening and closing her mouth without making any sound. She caught him looking at her.

"I'm sorry, Will, honest," Maisy said earnestly. "I didn't know, cross me heart and hope to die."

Will nodded and she was clearly relieved.

"You should've told me though," Maisy added.

"Twould have helped." Gruncle Maskall agreed and Will nodded. Then Gruncle Maskall turned to Maisy. "Twould have helped for you to finish listening too, yesterday, afore declaring your side of the room to be the new Rock of Gibraltar."

Maisy shrugged and mumbled "S'pose so."

"And," Gruncle Maskall said. "Twould have helped if I had been more forceful, mayhap. In making you listen. Howsumdever, I trust you, Magpie."

"Yes Grip," Maisy looked Gruncle Maskall in the eye this time and spoke loud and clear.

Will noted the names they used and smiled a little. Special names just like 'Gruncle',

"Now that I am on a roll," Gruncle Maskall sighed, "Will, tis best if you don't gwoan into the Wyrde Woods on your own. They are gurt big woods, mostly good but somewhen bad things can happen in there."

"Yes, Gruncle," Will said.

Gruncle Maskall looked at Granny and she nodded. "Words of wisdom, Fred."

He smiled at her and Will could see something of the younger man he had once been.

"By Geemeny," Gruncle Maskall continued. "I'm afeared I'm too old for this business."

"You'll scratch along, Gramps," Maisy grinned. "Can you fix Will's plane?"

Gruncle turned to Will again and reached out his hands. "Hand me those pieces,"

Will handed over the Spitfire and the broken wing and Gruncle Maskall studied them carefully.

"Gramps can probably fix it for you," Maisy told Will. "He's dead handy, ain't he? Made me a fine proper London doubledecker bus from wood."

"Really?" Will looked at his great uncle with hopeful eyes.

Gruncle Maskall gave a nod, "I'll give it a try after tea, Will."

Will felt a little bit better straight away and even more so that evening when Gruncle Maskall produced a box with wood working tools in them – the ones for finer work – as well as a pot of glue, paint brushes and small tins of paint. Will spent the entire evening in silence, his gaze fixed on each step of the operation carried out by his great uncle, and sighed a breath of relief just before bed time when the Spitfire looked as good as new.

"I'll hang it to dry," Gruncle Maskall said. "It'll be yours again tomorrow. Mayhap not take it outside to play?"

Will nodded. "Thank you Gruncle Maskall. It means a lot to me."

"I know what it is like to lose a brother, Will," Gruncle Maskall looked Will in the eyes and Will saw pain in them. He was reminded it hadn't just been Gaffer who had lost a comrade-in-arms in faraway Abraham's Kraal.

Gruncle Maskall broke the tense moment. "To bed now lad, chop-chop."

Will arrived in his bedroom to discover that Maisy had taken one of the blankets down from the lines, opening up the area around the foot of her bed. He smiled and changed into his pajamas. Burrowing into the snuggle of the blankets he heard Maisy say: "I'm sorry, Will, about the Spitfire. It ain't rubbish, wish I had one, I really do."

"I am sorry about invading your room," Will replied, after thinking about something to offer in return.

"So you bloody well should be, it is my room after all," Maisy rattled in a rush, followed by a softer: "Good night Will."

"Good night, Maisy."

8. A Bad Beginning

Brenda woke up slowly and stretched lazily. She wasn't usually one for dawdling in bed, but the previous day's journey with all its ups and downs had been very tiring. Eddie was still fast asleep next to her in the small single bed. Brenda smiled and ruffled his hair. Because of the blackout curtain it was dark in the room and it wasn't until she stretched out an arm to lift the curtain that she frowned; it looked like the day was well underway.

With a shock she realised that they had been due at their new school that morning. Brenda got out of bed and ran into the kitchen, but the black-out curtains were still drawn shut and there was no sign of life; the night's cold still lingered in the room. Brenda opened the curtains of the two small windows to let the light in and looked around for a clock, but she couldn't find one.

"Brenda. Brenda." It was Mrs Patterson who called; her voice faint and muffled. Brenda went back into the small hallway and stood uncertainly in front of the door of the master bedroom. Could she just walk in?

"Brenda!" Mrs Patterson was more insistent now. Brenda opened the door slowly and stuck her head in the room.

"There you are." Mrs Patterson was sitting up in bed. Mr Patterson was still asleep. Brenda could hear him snoring softly. The air in the room was stuffy.

"I'm not feeling very well this morning, Brenda," Mrs Patterson said. "Perhaps you could bring us some tea? Don't forget to bring in the cream and sugar as well."

"Mrs Patterson?" Brenda said in a small voice.

"Yes?"

"Do you know what time it is?"

"A little past nine, why do you ask?"

"We were supposed to go to school this morning," Brenda said.

"Well that's your responsibility," Mrs Patterson frowned. "Surely you don't expect us to bring you breakfast in bed. The deal was that your brother would not cause unnecessary inconvenience. You are to take care of him and your school arrangements, Brenda. Now please go see to that tea."

"Yes, Mrs Patterson," Brenda said and closed the door. She rushed into the small bedroom to wake Eddie up and get them both into their school clothes and then hunted around in the kitchen looking for something to eat. She found the remnants of a loaf of bread and some jam and hurriedly improvised a breakfast before ushering Eddie out of the door, forgetting about the Pattersons' tea in her rush.

She knew that they were due to attend the school in Odesby where they had been taken to after they got off the train the day before, so fortunately she knew the way. It wasn't that difficult: turn right after leaving the Hornsby Farm access road and then follow the much wider dirt road south until they reached the outskirts of Odesby, at which point the school was only two streets away.

The distance to walk was considerable and Eddie had trouble keeping up with Brenda; dribbling behind her on his short little legs. She felt sorry for him but they were already terribly late. Not wanting to make a bad situation worse she spurred him on.

She sighed a breath of relief when the school came into sight at long last.

"Brenda," Eddie said. "I don't like it here. Can we go back to Mummy now?"

"No Eddie," Brenda said firmly. "You know there is a war on, we will have to wait until it is over. That's just the way things are."

"Tomorrow?" Eddie asked hopefully.

Brenda sighed. "I am afraid it will be much longer than that."

"I don't like it," Eddie said stubbornly.

Brenda didn't like it very much either, but she had to set a good example. Pretending to be cheerful she said: "We'll just have to make the most of it, bravely and courageously. You are brave, aren't you Eddie?"

"Yes, very brave," Eddie nodded.

"Good boy," Brenda smiled at him. "Look! Here's our new school."

The trepidation Brenda felt when she walked into the school building was justified; it was a bad beginning. First she got an earful from the administrator when she had to register herself and Eddie. She couldn't produce all the paperwork he wanted to see – some of which he should have received from the billeting officer – and then he berated her for her late arrival.

After enduring that Brenda brought Eddie to his new classroom where the teacher lectured the both of them on the importance of punctuality. Eddie had tears in his eyes when Brenda was finally given leave to go and she bent down and whispered "Be as brave as Tigger" into his ear. A third reprimand about being late was given when she reported to the teacher of her own new class. The woman was irritated by the disruption and let Brenda stand in front of the whole class for a long time as she went on and on about Brenda's tardy entrance. Brenda felt awkward and uncomfortable and desperately wished she was back in Brighton once again, in her own school where teachers had always been pleased with her efforts and behaviour.

The rest of the day passed in a blur. Brenda was relieved when it was all over, and they could begin the long walk back home.

§ § § § § § §

To Brenda's surprise the cottage door was locked when they arrived. She had to knock on it several times before Mrs Patterson came to the door.

A nod was all the greeting they got. Mrs Patterson waited until they were inside the hallway before locking the door again. She caught Brenda giving her a curious look as Eddie fled into the small bedroom.

"People are…different out here," Mrs Patterson explained. "Better safe than sorry. I was very disappointed that you did not bring us tea this morning, Brenda. I did ask you to."

"I'm sorry Mrs Patterson…we were late for school, we had to leave in a hurry."

"A terrible excuse, please don't let it happen again."

"I won't, Mrs Patterson," Brenda promised and made a note to make extra effort to get up early the next morning. The last thing she wanted was to go through three sermons at school again, or disappoint these Pattersons who, maybe, would become more friendly if Brenda did her best.

"Please follow me into the kitchen," Mrs Patterson said and stepped in that direction.

"Can I change out of my school clothes first, please, Mrs Patterson?" Brenda asked.

"No," Mrs Patterson frowned. "You must stop talking back at me, child. I told you to come to the kitchen."

Brenda hung her head and followed Mrs Patterson into the kitchen. It was cold in there, nobody had stoked the fire in the kitchen range, which was meant to be kept burning all day. There was no sign of Mr Patterson.

Brenda noticed a pile of loose paper on the kitchen table, filled with writing.

"This," Mrs Patterson pointed at the papers, "is something I need you to read carefully. They are the terms for your stay."

Brenda nodded. "Yes, Mrs Patterson."

"Both Mr Patterson and myself are feeling very poorly today," Mrs Patterson said.

"I am sorry to hear that," Brenda said.
"We intend to rest as much as we can today," Mrs Patterson said and made to leave the kitchen. "Please call us when supper is ready."

"Yes, Mrs Patterson," Brenda replied automatically. Then she realised that Mrs Patterson expected her to prepare the meal, but before she could ask any of the many questions which popped into her head, Mrs Patterson walked out and went back to the master bedroom.

Brenda was seated at the kitchen table wrestling through the spiky letters on the papers when Eddie came in. He had changed out of his school clothes by himself and put on his cowboy suit which Mum had made from old blankets and a jute sack. Brenda would probably have to collect his school clothes from the floor, but she was pleased he had changed all by himself. She still had to get out of her own school clothes anyway, she would pick up and fold his clothes then.

Eddie glanced at the hallway behind him and then turned around to push the kitchen door shut.

"Swing?" He asked.

"Another time, Eddie, I have things to do."

"Listen to wireless?" He suggested.

Brenda looked at a small corner table where the wireless stood. She hadn't encountered the wireless in the words she was trying to decipher, though there were clear instructions to keep noise levels down at all times.

"I'll tell you what," she said, and then whispered. "We'll have to keep the volume really low, alright Eddie?"

Eddie nodded.

"Really, really low," Brenda whispered again.

"Really low, really," Eddie whispered back and then grinned.

"And if you hear the door," she pointed towards the hallway.

"Turn it off!" Eddie said triumphantly and Brenda was proud that he understood.

"We'll need a code word," Brenda said, "So that if I hear the door I can say it and you will understand straight away!"

"Spitfire," Eddie suggested.

"Spitfire it is," Brenda smiled and led Eddie to the corner table. She showed him how to turn the wireless on and off, tuned into the BBC Home Service, and then fiddled with the volume knob until she had a volume level which would allow Eddie to listen to Children's Hour without being audible in the hallway.

With Eddie installed by the wireless, Brenda returned to the papers Mrs Patterson had put out for her to read. Apart from the near illegible handwriting it was also composed in a confusing way, mixing household rules with tasks and chores haphazardly. Brenda decided that she would have to copy them out in her school notebook and organize them when she had the time.

They weren't to make noise. Brenda was to light the fire in the kitchen range each morning. They weren't allowed to play with the farm children (Mrs Patterson had added 'they all have lice!" to that). Daily meals consisted of soup or stew which was to be prepared in the weekends. They were expected to come straight home from school. Brenda had to mind Eddie and make sure he was fed, washed, and quiet. They were to be polite. Brenda and Eddie were to drink brewed tea, kept warm on the kitchen range all day, but when the Patterson called for tea it was to be fresh. Firewood had to be brought in, beds to be made, rules to be obeyed. It went on and on and made Brenda quite dizzy. She decided to go change out of her school clothes first and then see about lighting the kitchen range and heating up stew for tea before reading the rest.

9. My People

Will's new school in Wolfden formed a cascade of impressions, many of which passed him by in a confusing rush. The school building was in the very heart of Wolfden, an old low building with two classrooms facing Stone Square, a triangular convergence of roads with a carved standing stone at its centre. There were so many new Vackies that even half of them wouldn't fit into the school, so additional spaces were used as classrooms in the town hall and the church, both of which also faced Stone Square. The schedule was confusing, changed at a moment's notice twice already on Will's first school day. It also included a great many gap hours when whatever surplus of children there were in excess of the available classrooms and teachers lounged about on Stone Square, waiting for their turn at lessons.

Will didn't see much of Maisy because she was in another form but within a few days he met a few lads he liked and spent his gap hours in their company. They were from London but had been evacuated before the Blitz. They were fascinated by Will's experiences during the Brighton Blitz so on the third day he brought a battered and faded biscuit tin to school and showed it to them during the day's first gap hour.

The tin contained treasure. Metal which shone brass and silver; Will's collection of shrapnel and cannon shells. The boys were fascinated and huddled around Will, peering into the tin as he took out individual pieces and told them they were from anti-aircraft shells, fragments of bombs, or twisted remnants of downed aeroplanes. Will himself could recognize each piece and every one of them had a story attached to it. He transported his new friends to poor old battered Brighton so thoroughly with these stories that they didn't notice another group of lads approaching and surrounding them.

"What have you got there then, townie?" A voice interrupted Will mid-way a particularly harrowing adventure in Preston Park. Will looked up to see the looming shape of a bulky local lad with mean eyes narrowed in his broad angry face.

"Leave us alone, yokel," one of the London lads said.

"Scoot, clodhoppers," another one added and then yelped as the big lad delivered a vicious kick to his shin.

"About time you city milksops stop treating us Sussex folk all uppity," one of the bully's mates sneered.

The bully turned his attention back to Will.

"Hand it over, Vacky chuckle-head."

Will closed the lid of the tin and clutched it to his chest. He rose to his feet. "You're not having it." He said defiantly.

The bully shrugged and then without further ado delivered a punch that caught Will on his chin. The pain was bad. Stars danced in front of Will's eyes. The bully grabbed the tin from Will and pushed him onto the ground.

Will landed with a loud thud. For a short moment Will rested his head on the hard ground and kept his eyes closed. He heard the hyenas around the bulking bully laugh. Judging from the buzz of excited conversation they had drawn a public. Will knew that if he surrendered now he would struggle with the subsequent reputation for ever and longer. He sighed and then scrambled to his feet to face the bully.

The lad's narrow eyes betrayed triumph and the sneer on his mouth was infuriating.

"What do you want? Sheere-folk chucklehead?" The bully spoke loudly, performing for his mates.

"I want my shrapnel back," Will said.

"'Tis mine now." The bully smirked. "If you want it, you'll have to take it from me."

Will stepped forward, stretching his hands out. "Give it back."

The bully held the tin clutched to his chest with one arm. He swung with his other arm, his fist connecting with Will's belly. It drove the breath out of Will's lungs and he doubled over in pain. The bully moved aside with surprising agility and hooked one of his feet behind one of Will's and tripped him onto the ground.

Will went sprawling to the ground again, laughter raining down on him. He made to get up. Some of the onlookers dared to cheer him on.

"If you gwoan get up again, townie milksop," the bully growled at Will. "I'll break your nose."

It was clear to Will that the bully wouldn't hesitate to hurt him again, using his much greater size and strength to subdue Will. The cheers motivated Will though. Better to keep defiant than bow his head in submission. Besides that, Will was angry, he wanted his shrapnel back.

He scrambled upright and looked at the bully with fierce determination. Will stepped forward and said "Give it back" just as the bully drew back his arm and formed a fist. Will almost panicked at the sight but outwardly he maintained his calm. He clenched his own fists and brought them towards his chest. He intended to land at least one punch back this time, maybe two.

"Right, you asked for it," the bully looked at Will hatefully and Will tensed in anticipation of the blow he was about to receive.

"BILL HARE! What do you think you are doing?" a girl's voice suddenly sounded close by. Neither Will nor the bully took their eyes off one another, there was too much tension between them to simply stand down.

"I am talking to you," the voice insisted. The boy called Bill gave Will one last murderous stare and then looked sideways. Will relaxed, just a little, and did likewise. The girl who had given him a temporary reprieve came closer and for a moment Will forgot to breathe. She was about his own age and to Will's mind the most beautiful girl he had ever seen; with a calm serene face, bright green eyes, and a wild mane of frizzled red hair. She wore a simple white dress and was barefooted.

"Joy," Bill grunted. "We're just learning this Sheere-folk Vacky upstart his middling place in our Weald. Tis naun to do with you."

"He's one of my people," Joy said.

My people? Will was puzzled, he had never met this girl before, he would have been sure to recall such an encounter. Or maybe…he recalled the girl he had run by in the woods. Was this her? It might be. She acted like she knew Will. *My people.*

The effect of Joy's words on Bill Hare was remarkable. The bully paled and took a backward step.

"Do you recollect what we spoke about in Shim's Copses?" Joy asked Bill softly.

Bill nodded; "I am sorry Joy. I didn't ken he was one of yours."

Will was amazed. The bully towered over the girl and was easily four times wider than her, but she had turned him into a creature of pathetic meekness with just a few choice words. The girl turned to Will now.

"Did he hurt you?"

"He took my shrapnel collection," Will said, focusing on the worst of his pains.

"I was just joking, honest," Bill said and held out the tin to Will. Will took it without saying a word.

"Be off then," Joy told Bill. The bully nodded sheepishly before he turned and hurried away, followed by his mates.

Will looked at Joy with wonder. "That was incredible," he said.

"Bill will stay clear of you from now on." The girl shrugged and made to turn.

"Wait!" Will said. "What did you mean? *My people?*"

"That," Joy granted him a radiant smile. "Is for you to figure out, Will Maskall."

She departed, leaving Will in a mixed state of perplexion at the sudden turn of events, gratitude that he was clutching his tin with precious shrapnel, and heady exhilaration because he had somehow won the notice and favour of this enchanting girl. He did not know how she had bound the bully Bill to her will, but Will had no doubt that he himself had been thoroughly bewitched.

§ § § § § § §

"You want to stay away from that Bill Hare, dontcha?" Maisy said as they walked home after school. "He's bad news."

"I plan to," Will agreed. He was still aching where Bill had landed his fists.

"And you want to stay away from Joy Whitfield as well," Maisy ordered.

"Why?" Will was surprised, the image of Joy coming to intercede on his behalf had pervaded his daydreams for the rest of the school day.

"Cause she's my mate, that's why," Maisy decreed.

"Ah!" Will suddenly realised where the 'my people' might have come from. "But she was nice to me, I liked…she seems decent enough for a girl."

"I ain't having it, Will. And that's that. It's one thing you coming over here and nicking my grandparents and my room, ain't it?"

Will made to object.

"Yes, you have," Maisy stopped him. "But I can live with that, I've decided you're a necessary evil, Brighton-Boy. But you ain't having my mate."

"What if she likes me?" Will asked; confounded by the sudden increase of complexity with regard to Joy. He had been partially floating on clouds thinking of her but plummeted back to earth now.

"As if," Maisy snorted, then added: "You leave her be. She's mine, do you hear?"

Will looked at Maisy. He thought he detected something beneath her surface that indicated a panicky fear. She sounded very petulant, acting her size rather than age. Trying to place himself in her shoes, having her security turned upside down by the arrival of a complete stranger, Will decided that it was not wholly unfair of Maisy, no matter how much he yearned to see Joy again.

"Alright, Maisy," he said regretfully. "Joy's your mate."

"You bet she bleeding is," Maisy confirmed with satisfaction.

Will shrugged and looked at a carter driving his wagon along the North Woods Lane. He missed Brighton's busy streets and felt very much alone.

Maisy, however, was satisfied and switched to war talk, giving a spirited tirade against the Jerries who thought they could pound her London with impunity night after night. She followed that with a detailed description of the torture she planned for the first German airman to descend from the sky on a parachute anywhere near her vicinity.

Will didn't mind, war talk had been his favourite topic of conversation with Jamie before the Odeon had happened. Maisy would have fit right in with them in Brighton. Mr Hall would have enjoyed sparring words with her too. Mum and Gran would have been horrified though, by Maisy's liberal use of strong language. His cousin could curse like a sailor.

Will chuckled when he thought of the expression on Mum and Gran's faces if he were to bring Maisy to Brighton for a visit.

"And after I've pulled all ten of his bleeding toenails out of his feet with rusty pliers, I've got something that will have the blighter howling for his mum, don't I?" Maisy said. "I am going to…"

"Sing *Six Lessons from Madame La Zonga* at him?" Will quipped.

"Wasn't going to, but bloody hell, Will! That's a brilliant idea, proper jemmy."

"Plane engines!" Will stopped walking and frowned. Maisy fell silent at once. The distant buzz was faint but had an upward pitch and sounded deeper than usual.

"Too far off to know what side they're on, but heading this way," Will said. "They're flying low."

"Come," Maisy pulled him towards the wood fence of an adjacent field and started to climb it.

"Maisy, if they're Jerries we don't want to be up on a fence waving at them!"

"I know that, I ain't bloody daft," Maisy lowered herself on the field on the other side of the fence. "Are you going to stand there all day? There's a bomb shelter."

"Bomb shelter?" Will started climbing the fence which was easy because the parallel bars, made of staves cleaved from tree trunks, formed a neat ladder. He looked at the field and saw nothing but a few tracks of heavy wagons converging on the nearest corner, the back end of a hare which was barrelling away from them, and the shaws of trees surrounding the field. It was the last place he imagined any sort of bomb shelter to be.

The buzz was beginning to develop into a steady throb and Will followed Maisy along the fence and the tall wild hedge that rose in height to meet the lower boughs of a sturdy beech tree with a humongous crown. There was a structure of sorts behind it. Will was amazed to discover it was a small block hut made from hay bales. They rushed in. Will sneezed because the hay permeated the air inside. He saw a line of round poles resting on the top bales that supported the haybales which formed the roof.

"There's been horror stories about the Jerries strafing fields during harvesting," Maisy said as she peered around the corner of the door opening of the block hut. "Mostly women and children at work and the bastards would come roaring down and open up with their bloody machine guns."

"It's clever, this," Will said. He joined Maisy by the doorway and peered at the sky.

"It is, ain't it?" Maisy grinned. "Gramps has had the Home Guard out helping the ARP build them, the Canadians at Mordrove chipped in too after he and I went to have a chat with them."

"You've been to the Canadian base?" Will was impressed.

"Course I have," Maisy said. "I know one of the officers there, Leftenant Levesque, he's a mate of mine."

"Pull the other one," Will snorted. He focused on the intrusive out-of-place sound that was still heading their way. He had more than got used to it in Brighton but here, generally, it was mostly high-flying planes they heard, with the occasional dog-fight lower down as the pilots weaved and dodged their fighter planes. On good days a Spitfire or Hurricane would evade an attack by going into a corkscrew dive – seeming to plummet down from the sky before pulling up again just over the land, leaving the Messerschmitts struggling to keep up.

"They're Merlins!" Maisy cheered.

Will cocked his head and caught his helmet, which had been tottering already as per usual and now nearly fell off his head. Maisy had a good ear, the harsh drone indicated Rolls-Royce Merlin engines which had a sound like no other engine Will knew. He had heard all the German aircraft involved in the Battle of Britain pass by at close range. All but the Stuka which had been used over England initially but withdrawn after heavy losses.

The roar intensified. Will had no doubt that there were a large number of approaching aircraft. Each time the front plane reached a new mechanically induced pitch it was joined by one and then more followers, building up a frightful din.

Will and Maisy waited until they saw the first Hawker Hurricane appear over the treeline, flying no more than twenty feet over the treetops. The cousins rushed out of the block hut and both jumped up and down, waving and cheering for all they were worth. The sky filled with the crescendo of powerful engines blasting by as fighter after fighter hurled past in blurry streaks. One of the pilots spotted the children. He wiggled his wingtips and gave them a brief wave.

The flyby was over in seconds. The thunder mellowed back into a roar, to diminish into a drone as the Hawker Hurricanes passed out of sight.

"That must have been a full squadron," Will marvelled.

"Didcha see the pilot waving at me?" Maisy said, her voice hoarse from trying to outroar Merlin engines. "I reckon he fancied me."

"In your dreams," Will laughed.

"I'll show you," Maisy said with utmost confidence. "I'll meet a proper pilot one day."

"And pull his toenails out?"

"No, a British pilot. The German ones are butchers, ain't they?"

Will nodded but he wasn't entirely sure. He recalled Felix, hanging lifeless from a tree near his burning Junkers, a chap who inspired those words on the back of his sweetheart's photograph which Will had picked up from the street. Then he thought of Jamie and Mr Hall: Butchered. Before, he had talked just like Maisy did now and it was odd to recognize himself in her. Nonetheless, he had lost the surety she felt about the foe. After the Odeon all Will knew was that war was complex and could be utterly merciless.

Maisy removed the remainer of her blanket fort that night, a sign that sometimes peace was not an impossible objective.

10. A Breath of Fresh Air

Brenda was preparing tea in the kitchen. There was a big saucepan of stew on the range and she topped it up with some extra vegetables she had chopped and some minced meat which would have to simmer for a while. Then she cut some slices of bread and set the table, occasionally stirring the stew with a wooden ladle.

Eddie sat next to the wireless. He practically had his ears pressed against it to hear but he would be happily occupied during the Children's Hour programme, even more so if Norman Shelley performed Winnie the Pooh.

There was a knock on the front door, followed by more knocks.

"Eddie, Spitfire," Brenda said.

Eddie immediately turned the wireless off and slipped onto the ground where he started playing with Buntings. He was a good little boy.

"Brenda! Brenda!" She could hear Mrs Patterson calling her name from the master bedroom so Brenda walked into the hallway.

"Yes, Mrs Patterson?" She called back.

"Is that somebody at the door? Could you answer it please?"

"Yes, Mrs Patterson," Brenda said and sighed.

She opened the door a little and peered around the edge.

"You must be Brenda," a jovial voice said. "My Jer has told me all about you. I am Jenny Hornsby."

The woman who stood at the door was about Mum's age with fine laugh lines around her dark brown eyes and beautifully long raven black hair which she wore loose. Brenda was immediately reminded of gypsy dancers from the story books. There was something wild about Mrs Hornsby, though her attire was that of a farm woman, a simple dress and a practical apron. Her arms were laden with bedding. A girl about Brenda's own age stood next to her, holding an iron casserole pan in her hands. She had light blond hair and sparkling eyes which reminded Brenda of Mr Hornsbys. She had a slightly crooked but genuine smile and Brenda liked her instantly.

"I am Brenda, I am pleased to meet you Mrs Hornsby."

"This is my niece," Mrs Hornsby continued, "Elizabeth Hornsby."

"Everyone calls me Lizzie," the girl said.

Brenda smiled at her.

"May we come in, please?" Mrs Hornsby asked.

"Of course, I am sorry, do come in," Brenda said quickly.

She opened the door fully and stepped back, it was their cottage after all.

The Hornsbys walked into the kitchen and set the bedclothes and casserole pan down on the table. Eddie stood up to greet them.

"Eddie and Buntings," he announced and held his toy rabbit in the air. "Please to meet."

"A bettermost lad," Mrs Hornsby exclaimed with delight. "I am Missus Hornsby, your neighbour."

"Hullo, I'm Lizzie," Lizzie dropped to her knees. "Can I stroke your rabbit?"

Eddie nodded and presented Buntings to Lizzie. Brenda could see on his face that he adored Lizzie already.

"Mr and Mrs Patterson are feeling poorly," Brenda apologized to Mrs Hornsby.

"I bain't surprised," Mrs Hornsby said with a total lack of concern. "They often are."

At that moment Mrs Patterson came walking into the kitchen. There was alarm on her face when she saw Mrs Hornsby. After that she gave Lizzie a disapproving glance which caused Brenda to remember her comment about farm children and lice.

"Good evening, Missus Patterson," Mrs Hornsby said in a friendly tone. "I thought I'd happen by but I just heard you were feeling a mite squimbly, so we won't stay long."

"Good evening, Missus Patterson," Lizzie echoed her mother.

"It's been a long and tiring day," Mrs Patterson sighed.

"I understand, Missus Patterson," Mrs Hornsby continued to smile but Brenda fancied that she saw a little glint of steel pass by in those dark eyes of hers. "I came to bring some extra bedding for the chavvies, including a thick wool blanket. My Jer said that the ones in their bedroom were threadbare."

"Were they?" Mrs Patterson asked. "Well, I suppose it's very kind of you."

"We also brought you half a rabbit pie," Mrs Hornsby continued. That brought something resembling a smile to Mrs Patterson's face.

"Mr Patterson will appreciate that, thank you."

"Would you like me to make the children's bed for you?" Mrs Hornsby asked.

"That won't be necessary, I'll do it myself," Mrs Patterson quickly said, surprising Brenda. "I am very grateful, but if you wouldn't mind…"

"Oh, we'll be off now, Missus Patterson," Mrs Hornsby replied.

"Really?" Eddie asked, disappointment on his face.

Lizzie rose to her feet. "Would you like to walk to school with us tomorrow morning, Brenda?"

"That would be wonderful!" Brenda cried.

"Yes, please." Eddie beamed.

The Hornsby visitors departed with a flurry of goodbyes. Eddie caught Brenda's glance so he could grin at her and she grinned back. Walking to school, and perhaps back, with other children would be fun. Their anticipation was immediately soured though, by Mrs Patterson.

"Brenda, do you remember the rule about farm children?"

"Yes, Mrs Patterson. But we won't be playing, just walking to school."

"Don't you dare talk back at me." Mrs Patterson snapped. "You are not to mingle with farm children, do you understand?"

Brenda nodded with clenched teeth.

"Please bring this bedding outside to the scullery at once," Mrs Patterson continued.

"I thought you said…" Brenda stopped talking when Mrs Patterson gave her a withering look.

"You may use it after you have washed it. You'll start the laundry as soon as it's weekend. I am not having those things from the farm in my house unwashed."

Brenda took the bedding outside to the scullery where she deposited it in one of the coppers. She stroked the warm soft wool of the blanket longingly and then lifted it up to bring it to her face. It did not smell like it needed a wash at all, it smelled nice as if Mrs Hornsby had left behind a faint trace of herself at the cottage. A breath of fresh air.

§ § § § § §

Mr Patterson came out of the master bedroom when Brenda called out that tea was ready. He switched on the wireless before taking a seat. There was war news about the German invasion of Romania and some fuss about Neville Chamberlain's resignation from the House of Commons. Most of the focus was on the continued attacks on London and the furious war which was taking place over England's skies.

They ate in silence until Eddie ventured a hesitant "May I have some? Pie? Please?"

He pointed at the rabbit pie. Mr Patterson had taken a portion but not offered anyone else some.

When no answer was forthcoming Eddie gave Brenda a puzzled look. She returned a small smile and a little shrug.

"Children do not speak at mealtimes," Mr Patterson growled.

The rest of the meal was eaten in a tense silence with which the tinny voices on the wireless could not compete. He ate the rabbit pie all by himself.

11. Pervert and Spy

Will was in a world of his own; belly-down on his bed studying a small photograph when the door burst open and Maisy stormed in.

Will turned around, ready to hide the photograph when he saw Joy glide into the room behind Maisy. She had a serene smile on her face. Forgetting everything else in the world, Will stared at her; dumb and numb.

"What's that then, Brighton-Boy?" Maisy asked and snatched the photograph from his hand.

"Give that back!" Will protested and made a grab for it, but Maisy jumped backward as she studied the portrait of the beautiful young woman.

"Is this your mum?" Maisy asked.

"No. It's…it doesn't matter." Will frowned. "Give it back."

"I shant and this is Joy by the way, but you already know that, dontcha?"

"How do, Will." Joy bestowed a fabulous smile on him.

"Erm…ah…hullo," Will stammered.

"I told you he was a pervert." Maisy shook her head with great sadness. "Look at this Joy."

Maisy thrust the photograph in Joy's hands. "I reckon he is sweet on her, ain't he? Lost in her great big eyes, weren't you, Brighton-Boy?"

Will sputtered a protest but could feel his cheeks betray him with a tell-tale flush.

"Fancy her do you?" Maisy asked sweetly.

Will wanted to strangle her for embarrassing him in front of Joy.

"I can't read the words on the back," Joy said. She looked at Will, "It bain't English?"

Will shook his head and said: "German."

"I don't care if she's from…" Maisy started but then stopped. "She's a Jerry? You fancy a Jerry? You're a Jerry spy, aintcha? I knew it!"

"I don't fancy her," Will snapped at her. "I found it. There was a Junkers that crashed right in front of us. This belonged to the pilot. He was killed. I saw his body."

Maisy was impressed enough by that to remain silent.

"What do the words say?" Joy asked as she turned the photograph again and tilted her head to look at the image from another perspective.

Will had them memorised. "*Komm bald wieder und sei vorsichtig! Ich liebe dich.*"

"Do you ken what it means?" Joy asked.

"Come back soon," Will replied automatically; Gaffer had translated the words for him. Suddenly he sank into a dark pit of his own making. He clenched his jaws shut.

"Is that all?" Joy frowned and turned over the photograph again to look at the text. "There seems to be more."

"Be careful, and, erm…," Will developed a sudden interest in the ceiling. "…I love you," he mumbled.

"Do you now?" Joy asked and Will looked at her in shock till he saw that her eyes were twinkling and she was smiling at his discomfort.

Maisy laughed and then turned to the source of the photograph. "So you saw a Jerry plane crash? We've seen a crashed fighter, an E109, but after it came down."

"And his name was Felix," Joy said softly. "Poor them." She offered the photograph to Will who took it with a grateful smile.

"Right in front of me," Will answered Maisy's question. "I was with my mate Jamie. In a churchyard, fire everywhere, and ammo going off."

Maisy was intrigued. "This was in Brighton?"

"Luftwaffe all over the place," Will nodded, "I have cannon shells and shrapnel. The stuff Bill tried to nick from me. Do you want to see?"

Maisy hesitated.

"Of course she does," Joy answered for her. "Maisy reafes up on war stories, sureleye."

Joy stepped forwards and sat down on Will's bed. He felt his heart skip a beat. Maisy wrinkled her nose but then sat down on Will's other side.

Will reached for the square tin which he kept on the bed side table. Maisy's eyes grew wide as Will took out a shiny brass cannon shell. He handed it to Joy who took it and looked at it curiously.

"What is this then?" Joy asked, twirling the shell between her fingers.

"From the MG151," Maisy enthused, unable to contain her excitement any longer. "20 millimetre Messy-Smith ammo."

Will's mouth dropped open.

Maisy sighed. "It ain't just lads who know about these things, Brighton-Boy."

"Naun of that makes any sense to me," Joy admitted.

"The Messerschmitt E109 fighter plane is armed with two machine guns and a cannon," Will explained. "These came from a plane that strafed us when we were walking to the chippie."

"I got strafed too," Maisy said quickly. "In Odesby, but one of the blooming townies got the shell I had me eye on, didn't he?"

She eyed the 20mm shell in Joy's hands like a magpie, clearly eager to hold it, then continued: "Still no match for a Spitfire, wouldn't want to be strafed by one of those would you?"

"Not with those eight browning guns," Will nodded happily. "The Spitfire is the best."

Maisy tried a tentative smile and Will smiled back.

"Here," he took out another 20mm shell from his box and held it out to Maisy.

"Cor blimey! How many of those have you got?" Maisy stretched out her hand towards the shell case, then hesitated at the last moment.

"Don't be tessy," Joy laughed and reached out to close Maisy's hand over the shell. Her shoulder brushed Will's chest as she did so and her hair tickled his face and he felt drunk on her smell and warmth and wanted the moment to last forever.

"Bloody hell," Maisy said as she relished the weight of the shell case in her hand.

"You can keep it if you like," Will offered. The cannon shells were the second best part of his collection. Maisy was clearly taken by them though.

Maisy's eyes grew wide as she looked from Will to the gleaming shell. It looked like a giant rifle bullet in her small hand and Maisy's face betrayed disbelief at Will's proffered generosity and then distrust because it was a bribe of sorts and they all knew it.

"I got three of them," Will said brightly, then added shyly: "You can keep yours too Joy. Then we will all have one each."

Joy rewarded him with a smile, "Alike a secret club. The Covenant of the Cannon Shell."

Will grinned awkwardly, rather liking the notion of being in a secret club with Joy. Then he turned to Maisy.

Maisy became aware that both Joy and Will looked at her expectantly, waiting for her affirmation. Will remembered her vehemence about Joy being her mate to be left alone and hoped that Maisy would change her mind.

Maisy looked at the peace offering in her hand again.

"Well, I suppose the both of you ain't all that bad, considering that you're not Londoners." Maisy nodded solemnly. "One for all and all for one, ain't it?"

Will smiled and sighed a breath of relief. Attention then turned to the shrapnel in Will's box; especially his prize piece which had been lodged in his skull after the Odeon and had been removed by a surgeon. Maisy wanted to know all about that too. Will was sparing on the details, he didn't say much about Jamie or Mr Hall, and nothing about the sights and sounds which haunted him so, but told them the rest. He felt that he had made a big step in establishing a further peace with Maisy, greatly helped by the warm presence of Joy's company. He kept on sneaking glances at the girl to make sure she was real, marvelling at her close presence and apparent acceptance of his company.

12. Songs, Bombs and Laughter

Lizzie and five other Hornsbys walked past the cottage. It wasn't until they had disappeared from view for the last time that they waited for Brenda and Eddie to show up.

It had been very awkward for Brenda to have to tell Lizzie that Mrs Patterson wouldn't allow her to walk to school with the children from the farm, but Lizzie had just laughed.

"What do *you* want, Brenda?" She had asked and after that concocted the current cloak-and-dagger arrangement. Brenda knew that she was being deliberately disobedient but there was so much at the cottage that she considered unfair that it was hardly bearable, and the Hornsby children alleviated her spirits. The eldest, Leon, son of Mr and Mrs Hornsby, was near school-leaving age and tended to be a bit aloof. He had the same light-blond hair as Lizzie - all of them had in fact. Lizzie told Brenda that Mr and Mrs Hornsby had three children and that her own father Jasper was Mr Hornsby's brother. He had three children too, Lizzie his eldest. Their mum had died and Jasper Hornsby had moved into the farmhouse where Mrs Hornsby treated them all like her own.

The Hornsby entourage was generally cheerful. They liked to sing and knew a lot of songs from the wireless. They also teased each other continuously and

Brenda laughed a lot during the long walks to and from school. The youngest of the lot was Eddie's age and it was a relief that he focused on children other than Brenda. The walks offered her a momentary reprieve from all her worries and the continued tensions in the Patterson household where Brenda had to walk on eggshells all the time.

"Lizzie?" Brenda asked as they walked to school one morning. "I have an odd question."

"I like odd," Lizzie said.

"And weird," Eddie contributed.

"Yes, I do, Eddie!" Lizzie agreed.

"Have you ever heard of a place called Maskall Farm? It might be on the other side of the woods, I think."

"Will!" Eddie said. "Good."

"Aye, I ken Maskall Farm, been there somewhen and I've met Mus and Goody Maskall aplenty," Lizzie said. "Why do you want to know?"

Brenda smiled; she hadn't expected it to be this easy.

"There's a lad from Brighton," she said.

"A lad!" Lizzie laughed. "Is that why you seem so sad sometimes? A broken heart?"

"No, it's not like that at all," Brenda paused and gave it a quick thought. "He's like a big brother for Eddie."

"That's me," Eddie told Lizzie who smiled at him. "I like Will."

"There is a Vacky staying with the Maskalls," Lizzie said. "Howsumdever, Brenda, she's a lass, naun a boy."

"Are you sure?" Brenda's face fell.

"I'm sorry," Lizzie said apologetically. "I am sure, Brenda. Her name is Maisy, we play in the Wyrde Woods sometimes."

"Will is in the woods," Eddie said.

"Yes Eddie," Brenda hid her disappointment. "He'll be around somewhere, and I am sure we'll find him."

"Tomorrow?"

"No, not tomorrow, Moppet," Brenda laughed. "We have to go to school tomorrow."

"Let's not go to school," Eddie suggested.

"Clever lad," Lizzie ruffled Eddie's hair. "Howsumdever, the woods are full of Pooks who hunt chavvies during school hours."

"They eat children?" Eddie was fascinated.

"Pooks?" Brenda asked. "What are they?"

"Pooks are...," Lizzie frowned and then looked puzzled. "Pooks are Pooks." She shrugged, unable to provide a better description.

Brenda didn't like not knowing things, so she pursued the subject.

"What do they look like?"

"Faeries," Eddie said. He looked at Lizzie. "Right?"

"Aye, but we call them Pooks," Lizzie said. "It's the bettermost name for them, they don't like the other one. Can you say Pook, Eddie?"

"Pook!"

"Good lad," Lizzie beamed at him. "We'll make a proper Sussex man of you yet."

"The Little Man Who Wasn't There," Brenda said, initiating a game she had developed with Lizzie, in which they were only allowed to communicate using wireless song titles. She had been allowed to listen to the wireless at home all the time and had a good memory.

"Strange Enchantment," Lizzie answered.

"Jeepers Creepers!" Brenda said.

"Stop Beatin' Around The Mulberry Bush." Lizzie said.

"I Found My Yellow Basket."

"A-Tisket, A-Tasket!" Lizzie finished.

"Tisket, Tasket," Eddie echoed.

"That one didn't make all that much sense," Brenda decided.

"Neither do Pooks, I suppose," Lizzie said. "So that's fine."

Brenda agreed.

§ § § § § §

The school day progressed slowly and Brenda found it hard to concentrate. The list of chores at the Pattersons seemed to grow daily and she barely ever had time to catch her breath at the cottage. The only parts of her daily routine she looked forward to were the walks to and from school in the company of Lizzie and the other Hornsbys. Lunch hour too, Brenda reminded herself, for she had been accepted into the circle of Lizzie's school friends. Some of the townies were quite nice and their stories reminded Brenda of living in Brighton.

Brenda glanced out of the classroom window. It would be lunch break soon and that was good because the teacher was droning on at a pace and in a tone that was sleep inducing. Brenda had already got in trouble for falling asleep during lessons a few times. She didn't mean to, but she felt very tired sometimes since arriving in the Weald.

A convoy of army lorries rumbled by, on important military business no doubt. Brenda hoped they would drive straight on to Berlin and end the war so that she and Eddie could go back home. She would miss Lizzie but maybe Lizzie could visit her in Brighton, that would be good. Brenda cheered up a little as the convoy disappeared out of sight. She started listing the sights her friend would have to see. The seafront, of course, including the Palace Pier and West Pier but also the Pavilions and the parks and…

A high-pitched mechanical whine interrupted her thoughts and developed into a sudden angry roar just as the air raid sirens broke into their eerie wails.

"DOWN!" The teacher shouted. "Under your desks!"

The children scrambled down to huddle underneath their desks and the classroom grew momentarily darker as the source of the noise thundered by, heading towards the tail of the convoy which had just passed.

"Dornier!" Brenda heard a boy shout and then all hell broke loose. There were several oddly muffled thuds which were followed by deafening blasts which seemed to rip the very air. All the classroom windows shattered inwards and it rained shards and splinters in the room. All noise ceased after that and Brenda was puzzled by this as she watched the bright rainfall of glass settle on the floor in complete silence. It was a good thing they were under their desks, she thought, after which she was overwhelmed by concern for Eddie. Had his teacher reacted as adequately as hers?

Her own teacher was up and about now, her mouth opening and closing as she barked instructions, but all Brenda could hear was a persistent and annoying ringing in her ears. The teacher's intentions were clear though and Brenda let herself be herded out of the classroom to the playground behind the school. None in her class were hurt other than a few light scratches, but she saw some pupils from other forms stagger out of the school bleeding from nasty cuts. There was a bitterly pungent smell in the air. Thick black smoke boiled up into the air no more than a street away. The ringing in Brenda's ears continued though other noises began to be added to that: Teaching staff shouting instructions, pupils chattering or shouting out names, the air raid siren, smaller explosions stirring the clouds of smoke, the sirens of response vehicles.

The teachers tried to keep their classes together but this was impossible as many pupils were hell-bent on locating siblings and friends. To Brenda's relief Eddie found her and she clasped him in a tight embrace and then helped Lizzie find the other Hornsbys, none of whom were hurt. Rumours began to spread about pupils and staff injured by the flying glass though. An ambulance pulled in at the side of the school just as ARP personnel arrived. It was all very hectic and Brenda was glad when the pupils who weren't seriously hurt were told to go home and stay well away from the street which had been struck by the bombs. Looking at the smoke still rising there Brenda paled. It must be a hellish inferno there. She recalled what it had been like at a sweetshop which had been blasted to kingdom come by bombs in Brighton. Will had been there too, she wondered how he was coping now.

The walk out of Odesby started in an odd subdued silence but then erupted into a flurry of outbursts as all wanted to share their experiences of the attack. Despite the horrors unleashed upon them the mood then turned into one of delight when the children began to realise they had been gifted half a free day.

"You'll come to the farmhouse?" Lizzie asked Brenda.

Brenda was very tempted. The odds were good that the Pattersons would still be in bed, but what if they were seen? She shared this worry with Lizzie who just grinned.

Not much later Brenda was grinning too, when she followed the Hornsbys along secret trails that made use of the tall hedges and dips in the land to conceal them as they snuck past the cottage unseen to facilitate her first visit to the Hornsby farm house.

§ § § § § § §

"We heard the blasts, saw the smoke," Mrs Hornsby said simply when eight children trooped into her kitchen. It seemed huge to Brenda's eyes, easily twice the size of the one at the cottage. "Hullo Brenda, hullo Eddie, you're welcome in my home, sureleye."

"Bettermost not tell the Pattersons, Aunt Jen," Lizzie gave her aunt a look and Mrs Hornsby nodded.

"We've naun had lunch yet, Mum," Leon said. "Jerries want us hungry, bain't that so?

"We shall fight them in the kitchen!" Mrs Hornsby laughed. "Sit down, get out your packed lunches and I'll see if I can throw in a little extra."

The Hornsby children and their guests cheered loudly and then devoured the sandwiches from their lunch packs while Mrs Hornsby warmed up a whole rabbit pie.

Leon realised that the time of day meant that *Music While You Work* was being broadcast on the BBC Home Service. It played a lot of jazz and swing songs to motivate factory workers and the kitchen filled up with lively beats.

"'Twere meant as a little extra tonight, howsumdever, I'm sure Jer and Jasper will understand as we do have special guests today," Mrs Hornsby explained as she divided the rabbit pie into eight portions.

Brenda took a small bite and her eyes grew wide. "It's delicious Mrs Hornsby!"

"Naun need to be so surprised," Mrs Hornsby laughed, though Brenda could see she enjoyed the compliment. "You've had it afore, sureleye."

"Yes," Brenda said, quickly looking away from Mrs Hornsby's eyes. "That was delicious too."

"No," Eddie declared to Brenda's horror. "The strict man ate it all."

"Did he now?" Mrs Hornsby's smile faded. "Brenda, look at me."

Brenda slowly raised her eyes to meet Mrs Hornsby's. She felt her cheeks flush and knew that she had gone bright red for Mrs Hornsby was awfully nice and Brenda had just told her a hard lie. Mrs Hornsby held her gaze and Brenda's lip trembled. Lizzie, who was sitting next to Brenda, reached out and took Brenda's hand in her own to give it a squeeze.

"He did," Brenda confessed her shame.

"'Tis alright, Brenda dear," Mrs Hornsby suddenly smiled again. "I understand."

Brenda nodded gratefully and turned her attention back to her portion of rabbit pie, though the rest of it didn't taste as good anymore.

"Now," Mrs Hornsby changed the subject. "A lot of extra free time and chores to be done."

The Hornsby children all groaned dramatically.

"Aunt Jen," Lizzie pleaded. "Brenda and Eddie are here, bain't it? It'd be rude to neglect our guests."

"Aye, Mum," Leon added cheekily. "That's what my mum always taught me, sureleye."

"Well, I'll be…" Mrs Hornsby sighed and shook her head.

Brenda could not help but smile, putting that awkward moment of her dishonesty behind her.

Mrs Hornsby continued: "I feel as if I've walked into a trap of my own devising, tis unaccountable."

Lizzie and Brenda helped Mrs Hornsby clear up after lunch but Mrs Hornsby insisted on making everyone a cup of tea by herself so the girls could join the other children who were twisting to the Andrews Sisters' Rhumboogie. Brenda was sure the Pattersons would not approve and that made her spin round all the faster, laughing as she did. After they became tired they played a game of Tiddlywinks. There followed an exciting game in which everybody took turns to use their squidger to propell the winks into the air to score points in the pot or squopp opponent's winks. Leon won but it was a close call.

Then it was time for Brenda and Eddie to be guided back towards the cottage along the secret paths which Lizzie showed her, for Brenda's friend came along as far as concealment allowed.

Brenda looked at her, not wanting to say goodbye.

"There's A Boy Coming Home On Leave." Lizzie said.

"Wishing Will Make It So." Brenda answered.

"Deep In A Dream." Lizzie said.

"When Winter Comes."

"At The Woodchopper's Ball."

"In An Old Dutch Garden." Brenda finished. The girls laughed with delight, but then it was time for Brenda and Eddie to return the dour and sour presence of the Pattersons. Brenda was painfully aware of the contrast between the two households but the pleasant afternoon had given her the strength to keep calm and carry on.

13. A Grown-up Letter

The postman had delivered a package for Will. Granny Maskall handed it to him as soon as he settled at the kitchen table with Maisy for his after-school cup of tea.

"I wish people would send me packages, don't I?" Maisy said longingly. "My dad writes me all the time but all his letters get lost, cause Sussex is a maze more confusing than Tarzan's jungle."

Will started tearing open the package.

"Careful if you please," Granny Maskall said. "There's a shortage of paper and I want that paper intact and folded, bethanks."

Will nodded and took more care in removing the brown wrapping paper. There was an envelope inside alongside a flat rectangular box tied with a small piece of string.

Will opened the envelope and read the letter inside. When he was done, he folded it and put it back in the envelope, after which he stared at the box in silence.

"WELL?" Maisy burst out, unable to contain her curiosity any longer.

"Curiosity killed the cat, Maisy," Granny Maskall tutted.

"Satisfaction brought it back, didn't it?" Maisy answered. "It's true Gran, I swear it on the blooming London telephone directory."

Will untied the string. He opened the box and took out a sturdy but finely crafted hawthorn catapult.

"That's cracking that is!" Maisy said with admiration in her voice. "Do you know how to use it?"

Will nodded but didn't say anything, suddenly overcome by the memories that accompanied the gift; long rambles on the Downs where Mr Hall had taught Jamie and Will how to use the catapults responsibly and effectively. He bit on his lip and put the catapult back into the box after which he closed it. Maisy seemed disappointed that he wasn't intending to rush outside and shoot something, but before she could voice a complaint Granny Maskall intervened.

"Time for your chores. I want them done afore tea is ready."

Will and Maisy groaned in unison but got up and made themselves ready to go outside and brave the early evening chill.

§ § § § § § §

Farm work is a neverending story and a few days later Maisy stepped into the kitchen from the farmyard, halfway through another task she had been assigned. "Cor, it ain't half cold out there, is it?"

Will was leaning over the kitchen table, fully concentrated on a notebook. His brow was furrowed, and he was chewing on the end of a pencil.

"I hope that ain't one of mine," Maisy said as she pulled off her work boots. "I like my pencils to be in pristine condition." She laughed and then sang out the words "pristine pencils" several times while she worked herself out of her coat.

"Did you finish your chores, Will? I'm halfway done, aren't I? But I was freezing, need some tea to thaw out before I become a bloody icicle and Gran and Gramps are arrested for manslaughter. Doing them a big favour I am. Do you want some?"

"Manslaughter?" Will looked up in some confusion.

"No, tea, you Brighton idjit," Maisy shook her head and rolled her eyes.

"Yes please, thank you," Will mumbled and tried to focus on the paper in front of him again.

Maisy took two mugs from the drying rack by the old sink and carefully poured tea into them from the big pot which stood on the kitchen range, using a strainer to keep the soggy tea leaves from escaping into the mugs. She flicked the dregs back into the pot. The day tea was a rugged brew but provided sustenance on cold days which involved being out and about on the farm. Maisy carried the mugs to the table and sat down next to Will.

"So watcha doing?" She asked curiously.

Will groaned and banged his head on the table twice; letting it rest there after the last impact, a hopeless look in his eyes.

"Mathematics homework?" Maisy guessed.

Will raised his head and shook it. "Letter."

"The first one is an 'A', the second a 'B' and then so on until the 'Z'," Maisy chattered. "Don't they teach you these things in Brighton? I'm not surprised. London is ahead of things, ain't it? Best city in the world. Teach us how to read and write letters before we're twelve."

"Thirteen and no," Will said miserably. "I am trying to write a letter. But I am no bloody good at it."

"I am! I write my mum and dad every week," Maisy boasted. "I am probably the best letter writer in Sussex."

"You could help me," Will brightened.

"There's muck waiting in the sheep pens, ain't it? Got my name on it, or so Gran said."

Will's face fell. "Please," he implored.

"Alright then," Maisy conceded. "What is it about?"

Will hesitated for a moment and then passed her an envelope with his name written on it – the one that had arrived with the package containing the catapult. Maisy opened it and then took out and unfolded the letter. She began to read.

My dear Will,

I do apologize that I haven't written to you before. I spoke to your mum last week and she told me that you have been evacuated to the countryside. You must be missing Brighton as much as I am, for I am still living with my sister in Rodmell, but I shan't keep the house on Sussex Street. It seems that we are both to live in exile then.

"This is private, ain't it?" Maisy looked at Will who nodded.

"Just read it," he said, and Maisy continued reading.

I know you well enough to trust that you will make the most of it Will, you were always such a cheerful boy. Your family has helped me to pack our belongings and there is a box of Jamie's things waiting for your next visit to Ashton Street. I am keeping Jamie's Hurricane because those planes were his favourite toys and it pleases me to know you have the Spitfire. As a belated birthday gift, however, I am sending you Jamie's catapult. Mind you, it is not for you, I want you to keep it safe until the time comes that you pass it on to a new friend worthy of it. Jamie was one of a kind but he would have wanted you to make new friends, Will. I never approved of the catapults, as you may have guessed, but have to admit it kept the 'terrible trio' off the streets and Mr Hall was always in the best of spirits after he took you two to the Downs. "I am proud of both my boys," he would say afterwards.

"Cor blimey," Maisy stopped reading for a moment and wiped an eye.

I don't mind telling you that it has not been easy, Will. I miss them terribly and on some days it is not easy to put on a brave face. I would very much appreciate it if you could write me the occasional letter to let me know how you are doing in the countryside, it would do my heart good to hear from you.

Yours, G. Hall

Maisy lowered the letter.

"Well?" Will asked.

"It's a very grown-up letter, ain't it?" Maisy rubbed her forehead. "You'll have to write one back."

"I KNOW! I've been trying," Will said with a desperate edge to his voice. He indicated the notebook in front of him. Maisy pulled it towards her but there was very little to read; Will's reply consisted mostly of lines which had been furiously crossed out.

"So this Jamie was a really good mate of yours," Maisy asked carefully.

Will nodded. "There was a group of us, we mostly hung out in Queen's Park, but Jamie and I were always together. We went all over Brighton too, out of Carlton Hill and into Kemptown, the Lanes and over into Hove. And the seafront, always the seafront."

"And his dad taught you how to shoot a catapult?"

"He made them himself. Jamie's from hawthorn and mine from blackthorn," Will nodded and looked at the far wall. "He made a lot of toys for Jamie, including the Spitfire I've got."

"It's a nice one, well-made," Maisy said. "I'm sorry I called it rubbish."

"That's alright," Will said as he did almost daily because Maisy kept on apologizing for that particular incident. "He took us to the Downs a lot too. He was very fond of the Devil's Dike. And he clipped my ear once because I'd come back from sledding down the hill at the Racecourse in a frightful mess. Took us to the pictures all the time as well, he liked them as much as we did. Paid for it too."

Will blushed and explained. "Mum and Gaffer didn't have much money."

"Yeah, well, same for us on the Isle of Dogs, ain't it?" Maisy commiserated. "Sounds like you were there a lot? At Jamie's place?"

"I was," Will confirmed. "Didn't have my own room in my gaffer's house. Mum and I shared the living room at night. Jamie had his own room."

"I shared an airey with Mum and Dad," Maisy said. "Just the one room. Small too."

"Mrs Hall never made a problem about me eating there, even though they were on rations just like everybody else," Will said. "I sometimes felt guilty though, because they had better food than we had at home."

Will wasn't sure what had prompted him to confess so much confidential information to Maisy, but it felt good, like a weight had been lifted off his shoulders.

"Jamie was more than just a mate," Will concluded. "He was like…"

"Your brother, wasn't he?" Maisy nodded. "Some friendships are special. I had Sue in London. Missed her terribly when I got here, didn't I? But your Missus Hall is right, you can make new friends, they'll just be different, never a replacement. I got Joy now, here in Sussex, close as kin she is."

Will nodded. He had experienced moments of envy whenever Maisy and Joy's strong bond became apparent. They could speak without talking much like he and Jamie used to.

"Here," Maisy interrupted his thoughts, "have a look at this."

Will looked down at the table in surprise as Maisy pushed his notebook under his nose. She had opened it on a fresh page and had been pencilling in words even as they spoke.

Dear Mrs Hall,

I am very grateful for the gift of Jamie's catapult which you sent me. Also for your advice. It is true that I miss Jamie very much and find it hard to concentrate sometimes. I miss Brighton too, my cousin, who lives at my great uncle's farm, says I talk about Brighton a lot and she is very clever, much smarter than I am, so she is probably right.

Will looked up and Maisy grinned at him. Will shook his head but then turned back to the letter.

The truth is, I felt like Jamie was my brother and Mr Hall treated me like his son. So I miss my 'Sussex Street Family' a lot and treasure Jamie's things. I won't even let my very clever cousin play with the Spitfire even though she deserves to.

Will chuckled and then read on.

I should very much like it if we can exchange letters and as Vera Lynn sings: We'll meet again. For one day this war will be over and we can all go home again.

Kindest regards,
William Maskall

Will looked at Maisy and shook his head in amazement. "Maisy, you're a bloody genius. A-Maising."

"I know," Maisy grinned from ear-to-ear, "I keep telling you that, don't I? You can just use that if you want, copy it out, and even take my bits out because now you've admitted that I am clever."

"I'll use every word of it," Will promised, delighted with his grown-up reply to Mrs Hall's letter. "How did you know…"

"Cause I can listen too," Maisy said. "I'm not all mouth."

Will nodded.

The outside door opened and a brief draught of cold air blasted in as Granny Maskall stepped inside.

"Done with your chores already?" She asked.

"Almost Gran," Maisy got off her chair. "I was just about to go finish them, weren't I?"

"I need the both of you to pull your weight," Granny Maskall sighed. "With your gaffer off playing *sodger* at the Raven's Roost there's plenty to be done and he won't be back until late tonight."

"Yes, Granny," Will gathered his things together and stood up as well. "Why don't I help you Maisy? We'll have the pens mucked out in no time if we both tackle it."

"And your own chores, Will?" Granny Maskall asked.

"Not, erm, finished yet," Will admitted.

"Well then I'll help Will with his after he helped me with mine and that way we'll both save time, won't we?" Maisy walked towards the door to pull her boots on and Will followed suit.

Granny Maskall smiled, "By *Geemeny*, tis exactly what Liz and George always said."

§ § § § § §

Late that afternoon Will and Maisy came back in to scrub their hands and faces. It was nearly five and long before Will's arrival Maisy had contrived to convince the elder Maskalls that listening to the daily Children's Hour on the BBC Home Service was essential for her mental health; an arrangement Will thought to be splendid. Maisy was especially fond of Zoo Man. Although Will considered himself too old for it he did secretly like listening to Toytown; with Larry the Lamb, Mr. Grouser, Captain Brass, and many of the others who lived in that make-belief world where it was always sunny weather.

Granny Maskall stayed in the kitchen to prepare tea and Will and Maisy made for the living room where Maisy switched on the wireless and tuned into the BBC Home Service, after which she settled down on the floor next to Will.

This is the BBC Home Service. Hello children, everywhere. This is one of the most important days in the history of Children's Hour.

"Oh, we're in for a treat, ain't we?" Maisy said happily.

Some time ago we were honoured by the visit to the studio of the King and Queen, with Princess Elizabeth and Princess Margaret during the broadcast of the

Toytown programme. Today Princess Elizabeth is herself to take part in the Children's Hour and speak to the children of the Empire, at home and overseas.

"Cor blimey! Fancy that, a proper bloody princess in our living room!"

"All over the world," Will nodded. He was much taken by the magic of radio broadcasting.

Her Royal Highness, Princess Elizabeth.

"I wonder what she sounds like," Will said.
"Shhh," Maisy shushed him.
A high voice began to speak; the words carefully articulated.

In wishing you all 'good evening' I feel that I am speaking to friends and companions who have shared with my sisters and myself many a happy Children's Hour.

"Blimey, she doesn't half talk posh, don't she?"
"That's her job. She's only fourteen and sounds like a professional already."
"Fancy her, do you?"

Thousands of you in this country have had to leave your homes and be separated from your fathers and mothers. My sister Margaret Rose and I feel so much for you as we know from experience what it means to be away from those we love most of all,

Will swallowed and saw that Maisy wiped one of her eyes.

To you, living in new surroundings, we send a message of true sympathy and at the same time we would like to thank the kind people who have welcomed you to their homes in the country.

"That's my Gran and Gramps!" Maisy said.

The princess continued to speak about the children who found themselves a middling stride away from Sussex in far off places like Canada, Australia, New Zealand, South Africa and the United States of America. She said that she felt she knew those countries a little bit because her father and mother had talked about their visits to those places. The names sounded exciting but didn't mean much to Will personally, apart from South Africa where one of his grandfathers had died in the other grandfather's arms. He marvelled at the idea that somebody could consider a country's King and Queen as a dad and a mum.

So it is not difficult for us to picture the sort of life you are all leading, and to think of all the new sights you must be seeing, and the adventures you must be having.

"She's talking about me now, I've had lots of adventures," Maisy noted with satisfaction.

Before I finish, I can truthfully say to you all that we children at home are full of cheerfulness and courage. We are trying to do all we can to help our gallant sailors, soldiers and airmen, and we are trying too, to bear our own share of the danger and sadness of war.

"Me again; full of cheer and courage," Maisy remarked. "You're just a miserable sod, aintcha, Will?"

"Wouldn't have it any other way, Maise," Will said. He wondered if he was truly doing all he could to help the sailors and soldiers. He had pictured a much more active part for himself when war had been declared; usually involving the repulsion of the Wehrmacht from Brighton's beaches. Until the Odeon it was the rationing which had demanded sacrifice but now that he was eating proper food in much larger quantities than he had been used to that was over too. Will suddenly felt pampered and guilty because of it.

And when peace comes, remember it will be for us, the children of today, to make the world of tomorrow a better and happier place.

Will suddenly thought about Tommy Tickle and the clown's words about Brighton needing the likes of Will after the war and he smiled.

My sister is by my side and we are both going to say goodnight to you. Come on, Margaret.

Goodnight, children. Goodnight, and good luck to you all.

"Good night," Maisy murmured.

"And good luck to us," Will nodded. "That was good."

"It blooming well was," Maisy agreed. "Like getting a royal appointment for my adventures. I am going to get a sign made. 'Maisy Robbins, Adventure Specialist by Royal Appointment since October 1940'."

Will laughed at the notion, though he realised Maisy was probably perfectly capable of having it done and hung up in their room somewhere.

14. Toil & Trouble

Brenda woke at six am and got out of bed very carefully so as to let Eddie sleep a little longer. Brenda slipped her coat over her nightgown and made her way to the kitchen in the dark. She lit an oil lamp and then went outside to visit the outhouse for a wee. It was bitterly cold outside and she envied the Pattersons their chamberpots which they kept under their bed. Brenda would have to carry them out to empty and clean later. She filled two buckets with water from the well and carried them into the kitchen after which she went back outside to bring in wood from the shed. Back in the kitchen she washed her hands and face in icily cold water and then used kindling to light a fire in the kitchen range so that she could heat some of the water she had fetched.

Brenda lit a candle and took it into the small bedroom where she got dressed in her school clothes first and then woke Eddie up. Eddie was sleepy and not of a mind to be helpful so getting him dressed was a chore and Brenda struggled to keep her irritation hidden from the boy. Then she rushed back into the kitchen to intercept the kettle on the range before it would shrill its boiling point throughout the cottage. The kettle was large and cumbersome and Brenda took it off the range very carefully to pour the boiling water into the teapot.

She took a tray and arranged an embroidered cotton tray cloth on it after which she added saucers, cups, teaspoons, teapot, sugar bowl and the milkjug.

"Brenda, I'm hungry," Eddie said and stuck his lower lip out in a pout.

"In a minute Eddie," Brenda promised him and then took the heavy tray and carried it to the master bedroom. She set it down on a dressoir by the window.

"Shut the door child, there's a terrible draught," Mrs Patterson mumbled sleepily.

Brenda fled the room as quickly as she could and made her way back to her own bedroom where she made the bed and then to the kitchen where she prepared porridge and set the saucepan on the range. She stirred it with a wooden spoon with one hand to make sure it wouldn't stick to the pan and combed Eddie's hair with the other hand. When the porridge was ready she poured it into bowls and guided Eddie to the kitchen table and set Eddie's bowl in front of him. She put two of the bowls and two spoons on another tray and brought it into the master bedroom. She was hoping to take the early tray out with her but neither of the Pattersons had stirred yet.

"Please pour us a cup of tea, Brenda," Mrs Patterson said. "It's far too cold to get out of bed and I am not feeling very well."

Brenda did what she was asked, masking her anger at Mrs Patterson's remark and then fleeing the stuffy oppressive air in the room once more. When she got back into the kitchen she sat down to eat her own porridge. It was going cold, already the consistency of wallpaper glue. After that she prepared their school lunches and washed up the dishes and left them to drain and dry. She couldn't face going into the master bedroom again to see if there were any dishes there that were ready to be washed. Instead she checked to make sure Eddie had all his things in his schoolbag and then helped her brother into his coat so they could start the long walk towards the school.

When they got back from school late in the afternoon, Brenda made Eddie change out of his school clothes and changed herself too, making sure to fold their school clothes neatly and keep them out of harm's way. Then she went into the kitchen and prepared a slice of bread with jam for Eddie which he ate next to the wireless. She had to relight the kitchen range for the Pattersons had not bothered to replenish the fuel during the day and would no doubt complain that the kitchen was cold when they finally left their bedroom. Then she made fresh tea for the Pattersons and carried it to the master bedroom.

The Pattersons were in bed; Mr Patterson was reading a newspaper and smoking his pipe and Mrs Patterson was engrossed in a book. They didn't acknowledge her as Brenda cleared away the morning things and took them back to the kitchen. Then she went back into the master bedroom to retrieve their chamber pots and copper bedpans. She carried the chamber pots outside one at a time, trying not to look into them and ignoring the horrid smell.

The Pattersons were wont to use them all day rather than braving the cold to visit the outhouse. Careful not to spill any of the content onto her hands, Brenda emptied the pots and rinsed them out. Back inside she drew the black-out curtains closed first and then prepared the evening meal. Then she laid the table and waited for the Pattersons to emerge from their bedroom.

Eddie, fortunately, had learned to keep himself as invisible as possible during the meal during which nobody spoke as they ate their portion of stew and spread dripping and pepper on the last chunks of the day's loaf of bread. After the meal the Pattersons settled down by the wireless to listen to the war news; a daily mix of good, bad, and worse news.

President Roosevelt had been re-elected in the United States, HMS Jervis Bay had been sunk, Neville Chamberlain had died, the Italians continued to blunder in Greece and North Africa, the Soviets seemed to be on the verge of concluding a nefarious deal with the Nazis, and the Jewish ghetto had been cordoned off from the rest of Warsaw. Much closer to home, in a chilling vision of the future as it might become, Coventry had been attacked by the Luftwaffe – most of the city's centre reduced to apocalyptic rubble. It seemed to Brenda that the Axis weren't having it all their own way but she also despaired that it appeared the war was going to last forever.

Eddie helped clear the table and then dried the dishes for Brenda after she had washed them. Eddie sat on a kitchen chair and watched Brenda with a solemn face as she tidied the kitchen, swept the floor, and prepared the evening's cup of tea for the Pattersons.

After that she called Eddie to the sink and gave him a strip wash with warm water and soap, after which she guided him to the small bedroom where she helped him change into his pajamas and tucked him into bed. She read him a chapter from *The House at Pooh Corner*. Eddie fell asleep before she was finished. Brenda pressed a goodnight kiss on his forehead and snuck out of the bedroom. She went into the master bedroom and made up the bed, shaking out the pillows and making sure the covers were as neat and straight as she could get them. Then she went into the kitchen and placed her homework on the table. After stoking the fire in the range again she tried to get as much of her schoolwork done as possible, though in contrast to Brighton where she had always taken pride in presenting neat work, much of her school work was sloppy nowadays, and not always complete. Around ten she placed filled the copper bed pans and brought them to the master bedroom where she placed them so that the Pattersons could get into a warmed bed.

She went back into the kitchen. "Good night Mrs Patterson, good night Mr Patterson."

Mrs Patterson looked up with a brief flash of irritation on her face. "Off to bed then, Brenda."

Brenda nodded and went into the small bedroom where she changed into her nightgown and crawled into bed with Eddie. His small body was warm and comforting. Brenda sighed and closed her eyes, but even when they were shut, she could not stop the warm tears which rolled down her cheeks.

15. The Treacle Mine

Will struck down hard with his spade but hit a root. Pain shot through his hands, arms, and back.

"Blast," he muttered and threw the spade down, sinking to the ground where he huffed and puffed, wiping the sweat off his brow.

"Oi!" Maisy stopped digging and frowned. "Don't be a weed."

"I am not," Will answered grumpily. "Just need a breather."

"You're a namby-pamby Brighton milksop," Maisy said.

"And you're a London Mouth," Will retorted.

"Well yes," Maisy shrugged. "But that's a fact of life, ain't it? Nothing insulting about it; I win again."

Will glared at his cousin.

"What the *pize* are you two up to?"

Will and Maisy looked sideways to see Joy approach. Barefooted and in her white dress she formed a remarkable contrast to the two cousins who were covered in grime from head to toe and swaying with fatigue. Joy looked around her. Will didn't follow her gaze, he knew what she was looking at. They were in the Wyrde Woods, along the dirt road which led east from the Raven's Roost and which Maisy had told him was called the Forgotten Road. The area around them was pockmarked by scores of erratically located holes of all sizes, scattered around which were piles of excavated soil. Joy placed her hands on her hips and shook her head.

"Are you looking for treasure again, Maisy?" She asked.

"Sort of," Maisy nodded.

"We're in trouble," Will added.

"Moil?" Joy asked. "What kind of moil?"

"Gramps were furious, weren't he?" Maisy said.

"Mus Maskall? Tessy?" Joy sounded surprised.

Will could understand that, generally Gruncle Maskall was a man of infinite and gentle patience. Last evening Will had been mightily startled by Gruncle's eyes which had conveyed uncharacteristic anger. Now he knew that Fred Maskall could indeed become cross. Granny Maskall had been angry too.

"It's all his fault, ain't it?" Maisy pointed at Will.

"My fault?" Will fumed. "It was your idea, not mine."

Joy walked forward and sat down on the ground so that she was facing the both of them. "I hope you bain't thinking I'm going to mother a pair of toddlers pointing their fingers at each other, sureleye? Why was Mus Maskall tessy?"

"Gramps sent us to mine treacle as punishment." Maisy sighed and rolled her eyes.

"We haven't found the treacle mine yet," Will added.

"Not a sausage," Maisy confirmed.

"Mus Maskall sent you to find a treacle mine?" Joy asked, inserting a grave tone into her words.

Will and Maisy nodded, both looking miserable as they did.

"Must have been a gurt big trespass?" Joy looked pensive. "Chavvies don't just get sent to find the treacle mine for naun reason."

"It was…" Will and Maisy started simultaneously:

"…his fault!"

"…her fault!"

"I don't care," Joy said dismissively. "I want to know what happened."

"This one…" Maisy pointed at Will and wrinkled her nose. "…doesn't believe in Pooks, does he? Ignorant Brighton blighter that he is."

"Ignorant?" Will shook his head in exasperation. "You're the one who believes in Faery Tales, Maise."

"Hush Will, we don't use that word in the Wyrde Woods," Joy said. "We say Farisees, they don't like the word you just used."

"What? Fae…" Will was silenced by the need to dodge a clod of earth Maisy threw in his direction. Will glowered at her and then told Joy: "She said there was one at the farm…wait a minute, what do you mean? 'They' don't like it?"

"Just don't use that name." Joy frowned. "This bain't a joke, Will."

"That's what I told him," Maisy said with triumph in her voice.

Will stuck his tongue out at her and Maisy returned the gesture before she continued. "So I said we should hide in the hayloft over the stable, didn't I? That way we could lie low and spy, ain't it? Sooner or later Master Dobbs would show, I reckoned and then Will would believe me."

"See!" Will exclaimed. "It was your daft idea."

Maisy had explained to him that the locals believed their household fairies were all called 'Master Dobbs' and that Maskall Farm had one too.

"You tried to spy on Master Dobbs?" Joy asked, horror written on her face. "You durstn't ever spy on the Farisees. Never! Ever!"

"That's what Gruncle Maskall said." Will shrugged and rubbed his ear. "He clipped our ears, both of hers and both of mine."

"Four ears in total!" Maisy added.

"Mus Maskall should have done that dunnamy times," Joy said angrily. She turned to Maisy: "WHAT were you thinking? *You* should have known better."

Maisy shrugged unhappily.

"Do you ken what happens if you spy on Master Dobbs, or make fun of him?" Joy's eyes blazed the same fury Gruncle Maskall eyes had displayed and Will was too flabbergasted to raise issue with this countryside superstition which made the locals so volatile. Instead he avoided Joy's eyes and shook his head. Maisy must have felt the same because she busied herself studying a squirrel in a nearby tree.

"They leave," Joy snapped. "Lope from the house and more oft than naun they'll cause a shatter of mishaps first. Tis the worst of luck."

"You believe all that?" Will was incredulous.

Joy ignored him and turned to Maisy. "You recollect last Midsummer's Night?"

Maisy nodded, looking guilty and miserable. Will felt sorry for her, though he made a note to grill his cousin about this Midsummer Night reference.

"You don't gwoan mess with the Farisees." Joy insisted. "If you do, you're naun but a chuckle-head."

"That's what Gramps said," Maisy confirmed. "He said we needed to find treacle to appease Master Dobbs, didn't he? Two buckets full." Will's cousin pointed at two tin buckets standing by the base of a tree. "That's why we are treacle mining."

Joy's cloud of anger vanished and she laughed merrily. "Mus Maskall is having a chuckle at your expense, Maisy. Him and Master Dobbs."

"I don't understand," Will said.

"What did he tell you about the treacle mine?" Joy asked him.

"That there was a big mine, around here somewhere," Will answered.

"A big mine filled with treacle? Just sort of…growing underneath the earth? Treacle seeping from the soil?" Joy grinned.

Will looked at her with wide eyes. A treacle mine had sounded very reasonable next to Gruncle Maskall's steadfast conviction that there was a household elf at the farm.

"You mean…?" Maisy's eyes were wide too.

Joy burst into laughter. "Chuckle-heads. There's naun such thing as a treacle mine! Tis a tale for the little ones."

"Oh! We would have been digging all day!" Will exclaimed.

"And slink back home to admit we couldn't find the mine." Maisy narrowed her eyes. "He's been speeling us, Gramps is a sharp and a macer!"

"You got off lightly," Joy said, her previous anger briefly sparking back. Then her eyes lit up with merriment and she grinned. "But there's naun reason for you to go home empty-handed."

"No?" Will was puzzled. Gruncle Maskall had been very specific about his demand for two buckets filled to the rim with treacle.

"Do you want to turn the tables on Mus Maskall?" Joy asked.

As one the cousins replied: "YES!"

"Good, gather your things, follow me."

§ § § § § § §

Joy led Will and Maisy through the woods; heading south parrallel to the North Woods Lane so as not to be seen by any passing neighbours. It was a fair hike but as far as Will was concerned anything was better than digging pointless holes. They carried only the empty buckets, having hidden their other tools below some undergrowth to be picked up on their way home. At long last the path ran close to the broad dirt road and Will could see the rooftops and squat crenellated church tower of Nickleby.

They didn't cross the road however, instead they continued to follow the path until it opened up into an irregular clearing behind an old timbered building, a maze of outbuildings and sheds.

"The Earl's Barrel," Joy whispered. "Follow me and you maun talk, we must be quiet."

Will and Maisy nodded and dropped into the same crouch Joy adopted as she half-ran to the nearest outbuilding and then led them past fences and sheds until they came to the long back wall of a storage shed. It was lined with neat piles of empty bottles, most of them brown and without labels on them.

"Beer bottles," Joy whispered and then started carefully gathering as many as she could carry. Will was astonished when he realised they were going to nick them but followed suit, as did Maisy.

When their arms were full of bottles they withdrew out of the maze behind the pub and Joy led them on a circular path around the pub.

"So that we don't just appear from around the corner when we go to the pub," she explained.

"We're going back to the pub?" Will asked with disbelief. They had just nicked pub property, it made more sense to stay well clear.

"Maisy and I are," Joy said. "You're to stay behind."

"Why?" Will wasn't happy, he hoped Joy didn't think he wasn't up to it. He wasn't a child, he'd be a man when he turned fourteen and that was just ten months away.

"All-along-of them not trusting lads at the Earl's Barrel," Joy said.

"That's right clever of them," Maisy declared with enthusiasm. "Boys are useless, ain't they?"

"No we're not," Will protested. "It's not fair! Why not?"

"Somewhen the local lads sneak in the back to take empty bottles and then try to trade them in at the front for the deposit," Joy said happily. "They never suspect girls of misschief."

Maisy laughed and Will had to admit it was clever.

"So we'll get some chink?" Maisy asked. "How much?"

"Penny for each pint bottle, tuppence for those quart beer bottles Will took," Joy said.

Both Will and Maisy made a rough count.

"We're bleeding rich!" Maisy cried.

"We're thieves," Will muttered.

Joy shrugged.

"All for King and Country, Will," Maisy said. "There is a war on, dontcha you know."

Will didn't quite know how conning the Earl's Barrel was in any way beneficial to the war effort, but their deed seemed almost noble from this perspective so he decided to agree.

§ § § § § §

They solved the problem of Will's extra bottles by putting as many of them as they could in the buckets. The girls then left Will behind, concealed in a hazel copse, and made their way to the Earl's Barrel, laden with their loot. When they returned both Maisy and Joy sported wide grins and each clutched a handful of coins as well as the empty buckets.

Joy led them across the Nickleby road which ran eastwards towards Odesby and then through a thin screen of trees until they reached the railway track which they followed east. Maisy was ebullient and began to sing a soldier's song which Joy apparently knew as well for she fell in. The lyrics left Will blushing. It wasn't as if the terminology in the song was alien to him; Jamie and he had used most of the words at one point or another when they were in loutish moods. To hear girls using them, however, was another thing entirely. Will might have expected it from Maisy, but he had already raised Joy on a pedestal and she lost a great deal of the saintliness he had bestowed upon her that afternoon on the rail tracks. That wasn't too bad because it did make it easier for him to talk to her as if she were a regular pal rather than a beguiling enticingly beautiful forest nymph.

The girls noticed the songs made him uncomfortable and made fun of him until Will opted to demonstrate that he was savvy enough by singing a few of Max Miller's more daring ditties. Maisy and Joy liked them well enough and demanded that he taught them the songs.

Thus they arrived at their destination in the best of spirits, infected by their own derring-do and the prospect of getting back at Fred Maskall's little joke. The sugar factory was the first outpost of Odesby they ran into. It was located just accross the railway bridge; a bewildering complex of brick industrial halls, silos, a towering smoking chimney and heap upon heap of sugarbeets. Fortunately they did not have to navigate their way through the factory ground as the outermost building that served as a cargo rail depot had a rudimenary shop. This consisted of a simple table and chair and a wide variety of containers, most of them round steel drums. The employee on duty didn't bat an eyelid when Joy asked him to fill the two buckets with molasses.

"Pig feed, huh?" He remarked and Joy nodded.

The man duly tapped one of the drums and Will found himself grinning as he watched the buckets fill with a thick sluggish black substance. They handed over most of their money and walked back towards the Wyrde Woods; Will and Maisy each carrying a full bucket.

Maisy stuck a curious finger in her bucket and brought it to her mouth.

"UGH!" She pulled a face. "It's bitter."

"It's from the sugarbeets," Joy said. "You heard the man, farmers use it as extra feed, like gravy for straw or dry hay. The animals like it, it's good for them."

"Not like Lyle's Golden Syrup or Black Treacle," Will guessed.

"That's from sugar cane, not beets." Joy agreed.

"But won't Gramps be able to tell the difference?" Maisy asked.

"How often has he tasted treacle from a treacle mine?" Joy laughed and Will and Maisy joined in.

"Mus Maskall is clever enough, he'll work work it out eventually. And then he'll be pleased he has a treat for his porkers," Joy said.

"Long walk home though," Maisy said. "I'm famished, I am."

"No need to pass the Earl's Barrel," Joy assured her. "We gwoan caterwise, south of the Water Meadows, then cut across the woods, skirt the other side of Arthur's Fort and the Twin Hills and then Maskall Farm will be anigh."

It was still a long walk but Joy filled it with cautionary tales about folk who had crossed the Farisee. The one which stuck in Will's mind was that of somebody called Old Fletcher who had spied on three Farisee maidens bathing and had woken up blind the next morning. It seemed cruel to him and when he said so Joy laughed and assured him the Farisees had far nastier tricks up their sleeves.

Whether the Wyrde Woods were crawling with Pooks or not, Will concluded, it was best to give them a wide berth just in case.

§ § § § § §

Will and Maisy trooped in the Maskall Farm kitchen just after dark; looking genuinely exhausted because their buckets had got increasingly heavy during the walk back. Will was much impressed by the size of the Wyrde Woods, he felt like he had walked for miles and the woods had kept on changing their appearance.

"I'm bloody coopered, ain't it?" Maisy sighed and Will suspected she meant she felt much the same as he did. Anticipation, however, gave them renewed energy.

"You're late," Gruncle Maskall greeted them. "You made your gammer fret."

"And your tea is cold," Granny Maskall added. "I suppose I could try and warm it up for you."

"Hmm." Gruncle Maskall shook his head. "Tonight's tea was conditional, I recollect. Did you find the treacle mine?"

Granny Maskall tried to hide a small smile but Gruncle Maskall kept a perfect poker face as he spoke the words. This made it easier for Will and Maisy to do likewise. All their effort, the long walk to Earl's Barrel, Odesby, and back, was suddenly more than worth it because the expression on Fred Maskall's face, when first Maisy and then Will came forward to present him with a full bucket of treacle, was priceless. Will would never forget it for as long as he lived.

16. No Need to Worry

Brenda sat at the kitchen table, looking helplessly at a piece of blank paper in front of her. Mum had written her a long letter and it needed to be answered.

There was a little news from home in the letter. Brighton, Mum wrote, had been spared the kind of attack that had levelled Coventry, though not a week passed without sporadic bombs and strafing attacks, and Eastbourne had been hit very badly. Mum wrote that she missed her Brenda and Edward very much but was relieved they were not exposed to the dangers which led to an accumulating list of casualties in the seaside town now on the frontlines of a terrible war.

"We keep calm and carry on," was all Mum had to say about the situation at home.

Brenda closed her eyes to picture Mum and Dad coming home from work, tired and strained but there nonetheless and it made her miss home terribly. Mum was worried though, because Brenda had not kept her promise to write weekly and Mum's letters were filled with questions about the Pattersons. Were they nice? Did they treat Brenda and Eddie fairly? Was Eddie sent to bed on time? How was Brenda doing at school? Was she doing her best to be cheerful for Eddie's sake?

The questions haunted Brenda like accusations and she simply had to write a letter back. The Pattersons had informed Brenda that if she wanted to write letters home her parents would have to supply the stamps but Lizzie had told her that Mrs Hornsby had said she would be happy to provide the postage so that was one worry less for Brenda.

What to write to Mum and Dad though, was a whole other matter. Brenda thought she had become dishonest enough, by mingling with the Hornsby children, without adding new lies to her parents. She had already added a new falsification to the Pattersons when they had asked her if Brenda's family went to church. They had, with some regularity in Brighton though it was not something that had weighed a great deal back home. The Pattersons, on the other hand, when they did speak, inserted much godliness into their speech and just about every infraction of the house rules or condemnation of Brenda and Eddie's upbringing was on a par with a sin if the Pattersons were to be believed. Brenda doubted their words in silence. She was sure that God was kind and loving and would find little to approve of in the cold and distant manner in which the Pattersons treated Brenda and Eddie. Although Brenda couldn't quite put her finger on it, she also knew there was something wrong in the way the Pattersons complained about the simplicity of their transport to and from Church. Brenda thought it was awfully kind of Mr Hornsby to hitch a team to his wagon and bring them there in the morning and pick them up in the late afternoon again, for they insisted on attending multiple services. Brenda had gathered that the Pattersons insisted on getting out of the wagon on the outskirts of Odesby because they didn't want to be seen arriving in a farm vehicle and afterwards, they always complained to each other about the rustic discomforts they had to suffer. They seemed to hold it against Mr Hornsby that he didn't provide a more suitable mode of transport but as far as Brenda understood Mr Hornsby was under no obligation to provide any transport and was really doing them a favour with the kindness which seemed characteristic of the whole Hornsby family.

Brenda had felt guilty when she told the Pattersons that her family never went to church because the Pattersons had voiced loud disapproval of the 'modern heathen' ways of her parents and Brenda never meant to portray her parents in a negative light that way. What she did want was a little less of the Pattersons in her life. Despite their reproach the Pattersons made no attempt to rectify the situation. Brenda suspected that they were rather pleased to leave the children behind on Sundays because it meant Brenda had time to prepare the next week's stock of stew and soup, as well as chopping wood and tackling the huge task presented by the week's laundry which all had to be done by hand.

That still left one or two hours of free time if she worked hard. Time to be used to play with Eddie or, as she was doing now, writing a difficult letter to Mum and Dad.

Dear Mum and Dad,

Brenda stared at the page. It seemed so empty and she wanted to fill a complete page, at least. She had a vivid recollection of the shame she had felt when Mrs Hornsby had caught her telling a lie and had promised herself that she would never let that happen again with people she cared for. Not telling fibs meant that she could hardly tell Mum and Dad that the Pattersons were kind people who treated Brenda and Eddie well.

Eddie sends his love. I am taking good care of him and cheer him up as much as I can. We have our own bedroom and do not go hungry.

Brenda decided that leaving out information was a different matter. Not entirely honest perhaps, but it didn't involve telling lies, it just left out the truth. She figured that she needed to spare her parents from the truth simply because they had worries enough without Brenda giving them cause to worry even more. That still left a great deal of empty page to be filled with some sort of information though.

Eddie came to her rescue. "Write words about Pooh's wood," he suggested. "Then we can play on the swing?"

Brenda smiled. She had taken to roving about the farmlands and forest edges during their free hours on dry Sundays. Eddie loved these outings and was continually seeing landmarks from the 100-Acre Wood

in this copse or that shaw. Brenda was only too pleased
to oblige him. They would stop to animate Buntings
and Margaret Elizabeth with their hands and conduct
Pooh-like conversations.

*The countryside is very peaceful. Sometimes Eddie
and I play under a shady tree and there is nothing
but the rustling of leafs and birdsong to listen to. The
air is cool and fresh instead of smoky like in Brighton.
When we walk through the fields there are cows and
sheep grazing and mooing and bleating which is
nicer than cars and lorries hooting their horns.*

*Eddie said that the trees have been changing into
their 'autumn dresses' when all the leaves turned
red, orange and yellow and that was very clever of
him. The people in the countryside work very hard
and there are a lot of fresh vegetables and fruit. My
friend Lizzie took us mushroom picking. She showed
us how to find the right ones (round and brown) in
the top fields and we took them home and her mum
fried them with some bacon and that was very
yummy indeed. I have never tasted anything so
wonderful though Lizzie's mum makes very nice
rabbit pie too.*

As you can read, there is no need to worry about us! We do both miss you terribly and hope to see you again soon.

Brenda stopped writing and was very pleased with herself. All she needed to do was think of a good ending and then there'd be time to take Eddie into the orchard behind the cottage and push him on the swing. She thought for a moment and then added:

Everybody sends their regards.
All our love, Brenda and Eddie.

There! She'd done it, written a fib-free letter which would assure Mum and Dad that there was no need to worry.

17. Major Maskall

Will followed Maisy and Joy into the woods with mixed feelings. Though he felt less isolated and was pleased that Maisy seemed to be mellowing a bit he wasn't sure what to make of the invitation to come and play in the Wyrde Woods. What did girls know about proper play? He had begun to look at his new countryside surroundings with play in mind. If Jamie had been here they would have developed at least two score Robin Hood scenarios and half that many Cowboy and Indian games already. The Wyrde Woods seemed to offer a proper wilderness for such play, its potential far surpassed the Carlton Park Rockery Gardens which both he and Jamie had held in high esteem back in Brighton.

It was nice of Maisy and Joy to include him in their excursion but Will was doubtful that they could concoct any game which would stand up to comparison. He re-adjusted his tin hat and then let his fingers run along the reassuring smoothness of his catapult which he had stuck in his belt. What did girls play at in the woods anyway? Skipping ropes? Dolls? Mind you, he hadn't seen either Maisy or Joy with a doll before. Perhaps they could play hide and seek or catch, that wouldn't be so bad. More importantly, any chance to bask in Joy's presence was a boon and it was that prospect which had led him to follow the girls into the Wyrde Woods.

After they had walked some while Maisy and Joy brought their heads together and whispered secretively. They cast a glance at Will and there was a collective giggle after which Maisy increased her pace and began to distance herself from the other two, speed-walking ahead, clutching a mysterious parcel wrapped in a jute sack.

Will hesitated for a moment, then curiousity overcame his shyness in Joy's presence. He took a few quick steps till he walked alongside the girl.

"What was that all about?" Will asked.

"You'll see," Joy smiled mysteriously.

Will pondered the answer for a moment.

"Not good enough," he said, feeling very daring for challenging her.

"It is a surprise," Joy clarified. "It bain't one if I tell you."

"Please do tell," Will's curiosity was fully engaged now.

"My lips are sealed, all-along-of a most sacred oath of secrecy," Joy was grinning now.

"Now look here, Duck!" Will exclaimed. Joy looked totally bewildered and Will felt inexplicably pleased with that for his impression until now had been that she was regally and serenely in control of all around her.

"Duck?" Joy answered, "Naun yet, naun till we get to Willikin's Drove, just a few there, but there are dunnamy ducks on the Water Meadows in the South Woods."

"I was calling you a duck," Will explained.

"You were calling me what?" Joy looked incredulous, then laughed. "You're a middling scaddle, Will Maskall."

"It's meant in a nice way," Will protested.

"In Brighton folk call other folk ducks to be nice?"

"Yes," Will shrugged. He supposed it could be viewed as odd further inland. Even in Brighton perhaps, Brenda had never taken too kindly to Jamie calling her Duck all the time.

"Well, scaddle be meant nice somewhen too," Joy assured him.

"Scaddle. It sounds worse than duck," Will lamented.

"If you want I can call you duck," Joy shrugged.

"No, thank you," Will said quickly. "Scaddle will do."

Joy nodded and looked just a little too pleased with herself.

"Duck." Will added.

"Scaddle."

§ § § § § §

They came to a broad stream burbling contentedly over its rocky bed and followed it upstream.

"This is the Acsa Brook, it runs into the Rore River at Roreford, the ruined village along the Forgotten Road." Joy explained. "And here is Willikin's Drove."

She pointed ahead where the overgrown banks began to rise steeply on either side of the Acsa Brook. There was a narrow path which wound its way around the trees halfway up the right bank, but Joy led them deeper into Willikin's Drove along the dry edges of the riverbed. It was easy going at first on smooth stretches of shingle but the course of the river soon became more uneven. The sides of Willikin's Drove became steeper and reached higher, interspersed now and then with sandstone rock faces. The water in the river rushed faster along steeper inclines or formed small cascades where large blocks of rock had detached from the sandstone facades. Here the children had to scramble over the rocks or cross and re-cross the Acsa, hopping from boulder to boulder to keep their feet dry.

Will was in his element. This was true wilderness, like a canyon from a Western film; a dangerous route that had to be traversed without attracting the attentions of the Comanche scouts who wouldn't hesitate to dispatch Will with their arrows and then abduct Joy to bury her in a termite hill. Will retrieved his catapult from his belt and picked up a few pebbles. The Sheriff had tasked him with the protection of the rancher's daughter and he would sell his scalp dearly if they were ambushed. He alternated between scanning the trees and undergrowth on the embankments for hidden enemies and sneaking glances at Joy. She looked the part in this game; at home in the wilderness as she nimbly leapt from boulder to boulder or effortlessly ascended up the steeper obstacles. Now and then, as they crossed the Acsa yet again, she would be caught in bundles of sunbeams which set her red hair on fire and lent a brilliance to her white dress — causing Will to hold his breath, she really did look like she belonged in the pictures at moments like that.

They came to an area where Willikin's Drove zigzagged in steep turns. Will realized that this was the sort of place where he would have set an ambush himself. He loaded a pebble in his catapult and held it at the ready.

Joy turned around and caught him half-crouching, aiming his catapult at the top of the rock face to their left.

"Are you defending me now, Scaddle?" Joy asked with a smile.

"Yes Duck," Will answered, deciding that denial was silly considering his pose. "There are enemy scouts up there."

"You're being silly now," Joy admonished him.

Will felt a stab of disappointment. He didn't feel as if his play was childish; he had directed whole films of untold stories with Jamie and was just beginning to learn to do so by himself. Girls probably didn't understand that.

"All-along-of enemy scouts not daring to come this close to Wyrde Warriors territory." Joy's eyes sparkled like fierce emeralds and then she seemed to dance her way to the top of a cluster of boulders which formed one shoulder of a small waterfall.

Will scrambled after her.

"Territory? Joy, wait up! What is this about warriors?" He had to shout because of the water's rush.

Will worked himself up the last boulder and found himself at the edge of a wide pool lined by pine trees. Joy took some steps forwards, wading into the pool till she was knee-deep. Then she turned and lifted her arm to point to a large curved shingle bank along the Acsa.

Will looked. "BLOODY HELL!"

§ § § § § § §

Maisy came marching up the brook's bank and she was quite a sight. She wore a blue coat with yellow piping and epaulettes as well as a battered felt hat with a yellow hatband and some sort of insignia on it. She had an LDV armband around the arm of her uniform coat, a cap gun stuck in her belt, and she carried a bow and a quiver full of arrows. Some dozen children followed her. They were marching in two ranks. Like Maisy they all had LDV armbands as well as bows and filled quivers. The first bunch looked familiar and Will realized he had seen them around at school in Wolfden. The children at the rear looked wilder, they walked barefoot, their clothes had been mended time and time again, and all had wild straw-coloured hair.

"From school and the Hornsby chavees," Joy said to Will as the two made their way to the shingle parade ground to meet the procession.

The oldest of the group was a boy who looked a bit older than Will – one of the ones identified by Joy as a Hornsby – but most were a few years younger. The last rank was formed by two small ones who attempted to keep time with the marching but fell behind every few steps and had to scurry forwards to maintain the formation.

Maisy set in a song and the rest of the children joined in as they marched purposefully towards Joy and Will who had come to a stop.

Oh, oh, oh, it's a lovely war,
Who wouldn't be a soldier, eh?
Oh, it's a shame to take the pay;
As soon as reveille is gone,
We feel just as heavy as lead,
But we never get up till the sergeant
Brings us breakfast up to bed.

"LEFT TURN!" Maisy hollered and the marching formation lost cohesion for a moment as some marched straight, a few turned right, and the rest turned left.

Order was more or less restored by the time the ranks were near to Will and Joy.

"COLUMN HALT! RIGHT FACE! ABOUT TURN!" Maisy bellowed happily, but frowned when nothing resulted but a lot of confusion and milling about. "Turn to face the Colonel-in-Chief, you blooming misfits!"

This order was understood and the troop turned to face Joy and Will who was quite speechless. The girls had an army?

Maisy strode up to Joy with a determined step and saluted. "Wyrde Warriors ready for inspection, Colonel-in-Chief Whitfield!"

Joy saluted back and then indicated Will with her hand. "This one here says I look alike a duck."

"A duck?" Maisy asked incredulously and then whispered. "You're a right idjit, aintcha Brighton-Boy?"

"He's a scaddle, so he is," Joy said and turned to Will. "Bain't you, Scaddle?"

"Duck," Will replied.

"See?" Joy asked Maisy, who rolled her eyes. Joy added loudly: "Thank you Captain Robbins."

"I'll have a word with you later, Brighton-Boy," Maisy threatened. Will began to protest but she ignored him, whirling around and roaring: "ATTENSHUN!!"

The children straightened.

"This here..." Maisy indicated Will. "Is Major Maskall from Brighton, ain't he?"

Will straightened his helmet.

"Major Maskall has come to advise us," Joy added.

"I have?" Will asked no one in particular.

"The Major has proper combat experience," Maisy announced bombastically. "He's been shot at personally by Messy-Smith aeroplanes with cannon shells all over Brighton. He shot back at them too, with his catapult. Took at least two of the blighters down didn't he?"

Will shifted on his feet, experiencing a mixture of discomfort and welling pride as Maisy continued to list his Brighton experiences – magnified untold times by her lively imagination.

"What is she playing at?" Will whispered to Joy.

"Maisy reckoned you deserved a proper gurt introduction," Joy whispered back.

"This is Maisy's idea?" Will was surprised.

Joy nodded. "The high rank too, she doesn't just promote anybody above her own captaincy, Will. There's hope yet."

Will smiled. He shifted his helmet about some more and touched the catapult which he had stuck in his belt again.

"After the Major rescued that downed RAF pilot by jumping from both of those Brighton piers he always jabbers on about, that blighter of a Goebbels sent over his best bomber aeroplane, didn't he?"

The children were staring at Will full of awe and Will felt proud awkwardness as Maisy continued to embellish his reputation. "And this bloody Jerry cruises over Brighton waiting for Major Maskall to come out of the sweet shop. While he waits the Jerry amuses himself by strafing the streets and Major Maskall comes dashing out of the shop and saves half a class of schoolgirls, cross me heart and hope to die."

"What happened to the other half of the class?" Joy whispered to Will.

Will shrugged and grinned.

"So the Jerries send another Messy-Smith with a big bomb, biggest bomb you've ever seen, and drops it right on Major Maskall's head. Those of you at school in Wolfden have seen dozens of schrapnel pieces the Major owns, haven't you?"

The children from the Wolfden school nodded.

"Well they had to dig each and every one of them out of Major Maskall's skull. The operation was so complex they had a Bishop called Lewes carry it out in a fancy operation room in a proper big hospital. So now he is here to recover and advise us."

The children looked suitably impressed, except for the older boy, but he grinned away at Maisy without issuing a challenge.

"ATTENSHUN!!" Maisy shouted. "PRESENT BOWS!"

The children straightened up and held out their bows in front of them. The bows were all unstrung and longer than each owner was so it looked a bit like they were holding spears. Maisy heeled around and saluted Joy and Will. Joy returned the salute and Will quickly followed suit.

"MAJOR MASKALL, SIR! TROOP READY FOR INSPECTION SIR!" Maisy roared happily.

Will looked aside at Joy.

"Gwoan, Will," she encouraged him. "Make a gurt show of it. You know how to play, right?"

Will nodded, then beamed as he walked forwards for his first parade inspection as none other than the world-famous war hero Major Maskall.

18. Captured

Brenda watched by the door to make sure Mrs and Mr Patterson climbed into Mister Hornsby's wagon. She didn't close the door until the wagon rumbled away toward Odesby. Eddie sat at the kitchen table with happy look on his face.

"Secret Time?" He asked eagerly.

"That's right, Edward," Brenda smiled at him. "Chores first. As fast as I can and then it's Secret Time."

"I will help," Eddie stated confidently. Brenda was about to say "no" but then she thought of sweeping and a few other small tasks which shouldn't be beyond his capability. It would save some extra time; extra time that could be spent outside in the fields and the edges of the Wyrde Woods.

"So will we," another voice said, startling Brenda. She turned to see Lizzie walk into the kitchen. Lizzie was followed by tall Leon and the four other members of the Hornsby troupe.

Brenda's mouth dropped open.

"Lizzie! If Mrs Patterson finds out…"

"There's naun need for her to know," Leon said. "Lizzie said you need wood chopping?" He rolled up a sleeve and flexed his muscles, grinning confidently.

"Oh Pize," Lizzie rolled her eyes. "He spends an hour every evening looking at himself in the mirror, this one."

Although Leon was tall and big his face fell instantly, and Brenda couldn't help but laugh.

"Do naun," he grumbled in protest. "I'll go chop the wood now."

"Thank you!" Brenda was delighted and Leon went back outside. Lizzie spotted Mrs Patterson's chore list on the kitchen table and picked it up.

"Right, Brenda and I will sort the laundry," Lizzie decided and then rattled off a list of further chores which she allocated to the other Hornsby children and Eddie. In no time the cottage witnessed scenes of frantic activity as floors were swept, dishes were washed, stew and soup were prepared, beds were made, and shelves were dusted. The farmyard was much the same; Leon splitting logs outside of the woodshed, and Brenda and Lizzie boiling a wash in the copper in the scullery. The Hornsbys did it all in good cheer, singing *We're Going to Hang out the Washing on the Siegfried Line, Kiss Me Goodnight, Sergeant Major* and such songs as loud as they could, as well as taunting one another continuously.

As the list of chores grew shorter, the unexpected help started melting away, Leon being the last to depart after he had piled the logs he had split. Brenda went inside the house with Lizzie, shaking her head in amazement; all the housework that could be done was done now and in record time too.

"Thank you so much, Lizzie," Brenda said, shy in the face of her friend's generous gift.

"Don't worry about it," Lizzie said. "Ready for the woods?"

"SECRET TIME!" Eddie sang out joyfully and Brenda and Lizzie smiled at his enthusiasm.

§ § § § § §

Lizzie had another surprise up her sleeve. After they had hoisted Eddie into his cowboy suit, Lizzie took Brenda and Eddie towards the Hornsby Farm where her father was waiting in a light trap to which he had hitched two horses.

Jasper Hornsby looked totally different from his brother Jeremy Hornsby, whom Brenda and Eddie had met several times. He was far slighter than his brother and immaculately dressed, his hair combed and oiled and the ends of his pencil moustache twisted into long whiskers.

"I've heard all about you, lass," he told Brenda in a jovial way. "'Tis bettermost, by the way, if you don't tell the Pattersons about disyer trap all-along-of them naun doubt expecting me to be at their beck and call."

Brenda smiled. Jasper Hornsby had said it jokingly, but she suspected his fear was real and in her opinion it was not unfounded. Although it wasn't a very nice thought of her, she rather enjoyed the fact that the Pattersons would be rumbling along in the farm wagon this day while she, Eddie, and Lizzie took place in the trap which seemed to fly over the dirt road into the Wyrde Woods.

Eddie whooped with delight.

"Oh, do behave, Eddie!" Brenda admonished him and threw an anxious look at Jasper Hornsby's back. This simply was too much fun to spoil.

"Whoa!" Jasper Hornsby urged his team to halt. When they had come to stop, he turned and looked at Brenda.

"'Tis fine to whoop and holler somewhen, Brenda. I recommend that you give it a try," he said.

Lizzie laughed.

Jasper Hornsby reached out an arm to Eddie. "Would you like to ride with me on the box, son?"

"YES!" Eddie took the outreached arm and scrambled up the box before Brenda could even voice a concern.

She looked at Eddie full of worry as Jasper Hornsby worked his team back into motion, but then Lizzie's father folded a protective arm around her brother and she knew Eddie would be perfectly safe.

As the trap gained speed again, rushing on a wide forest lane lined by stately oaks, Lizzie grabbed Brenda's hand to get her attention. Brenda looked at her and to her surprise Lizzie let out a long "Wheeeeeeeeeeeeee!"

Jasper Hornsby whooped too, and Eddie joined in most enthusiastically.

"Go on, Brenda," Lizzie squeezed Brenda's hand. "Give it a try."

"Hooooooooo!" Brenda started a weak whoop but then, overcome by the fun of it, she followed it with a wolf-like ululation that was cheered on by Lizzie and her father, and imitated by Eddie. It was such a liberating feeling that Brenda did it again, this time screaming like a Banshee.

Then all four howled at once and Brenda clapped her hands with delight.

Jasper Hornsby slowed the trap down to a walk and began explaining to Eddie how he worked the team. Brenda could see that her little brother rested his wide eyes on the man and listened to every word that was said. That left her free to chat with Lizzie and they soon fell into their song title routine.

"You'd be Surprised," Lizzie said. "Bonnie Baker sings that."

"When You Wish upon a Star," Brenda answered.

"Down the Road."

"Only Forever."

"Scrub Me, Mama, with a Boogie Beat!" Lizzie finished and the two girls rolled around laughing.

"What the pize are the two of you talking about?" Jasper Hornsby inquired. "Is it a secret language?"

Brenda and Lizzie looked at each other. Lizzie said: "Yes" and the girls dissolved into giggles again.

"Oh-uh," Jasper Hornsby said in an ominous tone. "Moil."

"Moil ?" Lizzie asked.

"What is 'moil'?" Brenda wanted to know.

"Trouble, lass," Jasper Hornsby answered. He manoeuvred Eddie back into the trap's passenger compartment. "You'd best get back in, lad."

Brenda looked around nervously but all she could see were trees, mostly still oak trees though they were a bit less majestic in this part of the Wyrde Woods.

"Keep a sharp lookout," Jasper Hornsby instructed the children and then turned around to focus on his team.

"Dragons?" Eddie asked hopefully.

Brenda's worry was ended by a quick wink Lizzie gave her.

"I am looking!" Eddie said trying to look in four directions at once.

"What is that there, Eddie?" Lizzie asked and pointed at the thick undergrowth of a low rise to their left.

Eddie peered into the undergrowth and then his eyes grew wide. "Indians!" He said.

Brenda looked and to her surprise saw a whole bunch of warriors appear. They were festooned with feathers, waving bows and spears in the air, and whooping. They were child-sized and at first Brenda thought it was the other Hornsby children, but there were at least a dozen of them.

Jasper Hornsby urged his team into a light trot, so the trap sped up some and the attackers had to jog to keep up with it, howling fierce battle cries.

Eddie stared at them with fascination.

"Here!" Lizzie said. She reached below the bench and pulled out a jute bag. When she opened it Brenda saw that it was full of pinecones. Pressing a pinecone into Eddie's hand, Lizzie took another one and threw it at one of the pursuing attackers who fell dramatically, yelping in pain and clutching a make-belief wound. Eddie understood the point of the game in an instant and began to throw pinecones at them with relish, cheering every hit. There was no end to foes, because all who fell would rise again and resume running once the last of the living had run past them. Lizzie and Brenda threw a dozen cones each but left the greater part of the supply in the bag for Eddie who was having the time of his life.

When the bag was empty Lizzie shouted: "Dad! We're out of ammo!"

Jasper Hornsby clucked his horses – the beasts not the least bit impressed by all the hullaballoo – to a halt. "Alas, we must surrender," he announced calmly.

Brenda noticed that he stayed on the box unmolested as she, Lizzie, and Eddie were hauled out of the trap by the jubilant attackers and dragged away into the Wyrde Woods. Lizzie struggled and insulted her captors, Eddie grinned away at them, and Brenda felt oddly free for a captive.

19. Chasing Simon and Nancy

Will stopped for a moment to catch his breath.

"Try to keep up with us, Will!" Joy called out cheerfully.

"You are slowing us down, Brighton-Boy!" Maisy sang out with delight in her voice.

Will grumbled an incoherent reply and gave Simon and Nancy a foul look. It was all their fault. The two stood just beyond his reach, looking at him calmly while they waited for the fun to commence again.

The whole misadventure had started early in the morning when Joy had taken Will and Maisy to the location of a proposed fort, near the cottage where she lived. Although Will was adamant in his belief that girls couldn't possibly build a fort properly, he had tagged along presuming they might need his expertise.

When shown a mass of tough and hardy autumn green at the edge of a clearing in the woods near Joy's home he had been dismissive. There were glimpses of faded sandstone to be sure, but mostly he had seen an impregnable tangle of saplings, bushes, and weeds. How could they even begin to clear that?

"With proper tools," Joy had smiled mysteriously, after which she had led them back to her cottage which was called The Owlery.

To Will's consternation Joy had orchestrated a most peculiar procession there. Maisy had been allocated three alarmingly large pigs which Joy had released from their pens. The largest of them had circled Maisy and then drove its lowered head between Maisy's knees after which the creature had moved its head up, thereby lifting Maisy off the ground and onto its neck.

Will had been about to call out in alarm when Maisy had giggled and shifted backwards to take place on the pig's back with a hearty: "Hullo, Bacon me old girl!"

Bacon had oinked at length in response. It wouldn't surprise Will if the two had actually been talking; Maisy had a gift with animals.

Joy had then added six goats to the column. These weren't frolicking kids, but adults with dirty matted coats and foul expressions. All of them exuded a strong musty smell.

"I'll take four," Joy had decided. "Do you think you can manage Simon and Nancy, Will?"

"Of course," Will had pronounced bravely.

He regretted that confidence now though because it had become quite clear to him that goat-herding was not his calling. Maisy led the procession, still riding Bacon. The two other pigs, called Rye and Whitfield, ambled behind Bacon most agreeably. As far as Will could see Maisy wasn't doing any work at all but most voluble in claiming credit for the smooth progress of her vanguard. Joy followed and seemed to have no trouble keeping her four goats under control. She had found a long thin sprig and whenever one of the goats made an escape attempt she'd tut and flick undergrowth or low-hanging branches in front of the escapee after which the goat would obediently step back into the line which was slowly weaving its way through the trees.

Will formed the rear guard with Simon and Nancy but his companions showed no inclination to listen to his instructions. On the contrary, they seemed intent on sabotaging every step of the way. At first Will had thought they were a bit dim-witted and simply didn't understand what he wanted them to do. By now he realised they were evil cunning creatures who knew exactly what they were doing. They acted in concord with each other in crafty ways; dashing off to the left or right one at a time. Will would set off in pursuit, but whenever he had managed to catch up with either Simon or Nancy and driven the goat back to their station at the back of the column, the other would bleat defiantly and make a run for it.

Will was quite tired already from all the running to and fro, and demotivated even further by the fact that he was being continually outsmarted by two smelly goats.

"Will?" Joy's voice again, with some concern in it this time.

"Coming!" Will shouted back, refusing to concede defeat. He picked up a long hazel switch and tried to flick it at some undergrowth near Nancy, as he had seen Joy do. Nancy bleated a protest and stepped out of reach – in the wrong direction of course. Will took a few steps forward, but Nancy continued to nimbly foot herself out of his reach. In doing so, she distracted Will's attention away from Simon who circled the boy and then lowered his head. The first indication Will had that he was being charged by a billy-goat was when Simon's rounded horns made a sudden impact with Will's bottom and the boy was thrown to the ground. The fall knocked the breath out of him and for a moment Will lay there stunned. When he scrambled up again, he turned around, ready to give Simon a piece of his mind. Will was rendered speechless, however, by the sight of Simon looking at him calmly as the goat happily chewed on Will's switch.

"Give that to me, that's mine," Will lurched forward but Simon turned, the switch still in his mouth, and dashed into the forest. Will set off in pursuit but the goat was fast and agile, especially after discarding the hazel branch when it was neatly chewed into halves. Simon then chose a particularly obstructive patch of undergrowth which barely impeded the goat's momentum but hooked, entangled, and whipped Will most mercilessly. The boy continued chasing the goat with dogged determination, even as Simon increased the distance between them. The merry dance the billy-goat led Will in left the boy thoroughly disorientated. Just as Will had begun to fear that he was lost he stumbled into the small clearing where they had left Nancy; Simon had evidently circled back.

Will came to a halt and stared angrily at the two goats. They looked back calmly; their yellow eyes with the odd horizontal black barred pupils inscrutable, though Will could swear they were grinning at him. Just as he caught his breath, Simon and Nancy took off simultaneously in two different directions, forcing Will to dash headlong into another fruitless pursuit.

Some ten minutes later he stumbled into the large clearing where Joy and Maisy were waiting for him. Will was gasping for breath and sweating. His face and the back of his hands were covered in scratches. His hair sported twigs and leaves. The girls laughed at the sight of him.

Will took a deep breath to gather the courage to confess that he had lost his two charges when he noticed Simon and Nancy standing behind Joy. The goats gave him triumphant looks and Will scowled at them.

"Useless in Brighton, aren't they?" Maisy shook her head. "No wonder London is ten times better, ain't it?"

"Is not," Will managed to utter and then dropped onto the grass and rolled onto his back.

"You're right," Maisy conceded. "London is a *hundred* times better. I got me pigs here no problem, didn't I?"

Will glowered at her.

"Stop being a scrowse, Will. You're both in the Wyrde Woods now, naun in Lunnon or Brighton," Joy said. "Take some rest, Scaddle. The hard work is done now."

Will nodded gratefully and stared at the few clouds sailing overhead. Ignoring the girls and animals for a little while suited him just fine; in fact, he never wanted to lay his eyes on a goat ever again. Devising ingenious ways to avenge his pride on Simon and Nancy, he dozed off.

§   §   §   §   §   §   §

Will dreamed of seagulls wheeling and gliding over a green sea which sent its waves crashing on a shingle beach; the water hissing and pebbles rattling as the waves withdrew. He was looking for rounded pebbles for his catapult and found the finest samples but kept on dropping them and having to look for them all over again. Just as he had finally succeeded in filling both his hands with the best finds, his nose started to itch. He struggled to ignore the itch but it refused to go away till at last, exasperated, he dropped the pebbles to scratch his nose. A voice called, seemingly from far away.

"Will?"

"Ammo." Will heard his own voice as he fought to stay in his dream, wanting his rounded pebbles back. His nose itched again.

"You've been asleep for hours, Scaddle. Time to wake up."

A girl's voice. Joy.

Will slowly opened his eyes and his vision was filled with Joy, because she was leaning over him, a smile on

175

her lovely face and a long blade of grass in her hands with which she tickled his nose.

"Did I miss something, Duck?" Will mumbled; the cries of the seagulls and crash of the waves fading from his mind.

Joy brought her mouth close to his ear and whispered: "Magic."

Will felt her breath brush his ear and was suddenly wide awake; simultaneously delighted and alarmed by Joy's proximity. It was as if they were the only ones in the whole wide world and that was a wonderful feeling, but Will panicked and scrambled backwards and sat up.

"Lazy Brightonian, letting us do all the work," Maisy appeared in his vision.

Will ignored his cousin. He dearly wanted to hang on to the enchantment of Joy's bright green eyes and sweet breath for a few more moments, but his eyes were drawn by a mighty spectacle in the clearing, behind calmly grazing pigs and goats.

Stunned, Will rose to his feet and took slow uncertain steps forward.

The green barrier which he had seen that morning had vanished almost entirely, exposing a hodgepodge of sandstone walls. As Will wandered closer he began to see logic in the jumble of smooth-faced walls. The ones closer by were irregular in height; rising up two to three feet, but behind that the walls grew up to five and even six feet. As he reached the edge of the ruins, Will could see that the walls formed neat rectangular patterns and he could make out doorways connecting room after room.

He turned to Joy and Maisy, who had followed him, expectation on their faces.

"How…?" Will shook his head in disbelief. Joy had said 'magic' and it certainly appeared like it to him.

"The goats and pigs, ain't it?" Maisy declared. "They were dead hungry, cleared the ruins."

Will shook his head again.

"Well?" Joy asked. "Do you think it will make a fine fort, or naun? We'll have to stamp the ground some; the porkers rooted it up, sureleye."

Will turned to face the ruins, eager to explore the chambers within.

"It's just perfect, just perfect," he said with admiration in his voice.

The girls beamed.

20. The Royal Palace

Brenda, Eddie, and Lizzie were herded along a dirt road which passed through the remnants of an ancient village, its skeletal remains rising up eerily from beds of ivy, and then along a path which led steadily upwards until they came to a brook which the captors and their captives followed into the woods. After a while they reached a building with stout stone walls and a crudely thatched flat roof over the higher parts, as well as a thatched overhang resting on uprights secured to the nearer lower walls.

"The Royal Palace," one of the captors said dramatically, as he indicated it with his hand.

Brenda pursed her lips; they had obviously never seen the domes and spires of Brighton Pavilions. Eddie nodded full of conviction though, so Brenda played along.

"Why have you brought us to this magnificent palace?" She demanded to know.

"No speaking!" One of the captors reprimanded her, then he ordered the rest: "Take them to the throne room!"

The prisoners were herded into the building and passed through two rooms before finding themselves into a large room at the back. The first rooms had been dark but the roof in the back room had hatches built into it which were opened to let daylight in. At the other end of the room, by another doorway, a dais had been built from earth and logs, draped with old blankets. Two girls reclined on the dais, lying on their side and supporting themselves on one elbow, wrapped in old bed sheets. One looked about seven or eight years old, the other much older than Brenda, probably twelve or thirteen.

The warriors crowded into the room and formed lines along the walls, leaving Brenda and her companions facing the two girls on the dais.

"Who are you!" Lizzie shouted at them.

Eddie nodded, he wanted to know too.

The younger girl waved regally at the nearest warrior who answered Lizzie's question.

"Behold Cleo! Behold Patra! QUEENS OF EGYPT!"

"Pssst, you forgot to say Sheba," the youngest Queen of Egypt hissed at the warrior.

"AND SHEBA!" The warrior hollered dutifully.

"Why Sheba?" The older Queen of Egypt and Sheba asked.

"Cause it sounds dead impressive, dunnit?" the younger Queen of Egypt and Sheba answered her.

Lizzie dropped to her knees and fell to the ground. "Hail to the Queens of Egypt and Sheba!" She shouted.

Eddie and Brenda dropped to their knees too.

"Queens of Gypt and Sheebah!" Eddie echoed Lizzie and threw himself on the ground as well.

Brenda thought being on her knees was deferential enough and stayed there.

"Why were these cretins arrested?" The younger Queen of Egypt and Sheba demanded to know.

"Treason, your Majesty, plotting against the Roman Empire," one of the warriors spoke up.

"Plotting against the Romans?" Leon Hornsby marched in from the other door, draped in a white bedsheet and wearing a holly crown.

"HAIL JULES CEASAR!" The warriors bellowed as one.

Brenda raised an eyebrow and shook her head.

"Fetch me that one!" Leon pointed at Lizzie.

"Aye, Jules Ceasar, drackly," one of the warriors said, after which Lizzie was seized and dragged to the dais.

"Were you plotting against Rome, wench?" Leon asked imperiously.

"Only a little bit," Lizzie admitted.

"FEED HER TO THE LIONS!" Leon hollered and the warriors took hold of Lizzie again, but she struggled and begged most earnestly for mercy.

"Stop!" The younger Queen of Egypt and Sheba shouted. "I feel sorry for her."

"Thank you, thank you!" Lizzie said.

"Feed her to the CROCODILES instead, ain't it?" The young queen ordered.

Lizzie was seized again and escorted out of the throne room kicking and screaming.

"You there," the older Queen of Egypt and Sheba pointed at Eddie. "Who are you."

Eddie bravely marched forward. "Edward. Pleased to meet."

"A royal name!" The older queen pronounced regally. "A squire to serve us!"

"I can be a squire?" Eddie asked eagerly.

The older queen nodded. One of the warriors gave Eddie a pine branch to hold over the Queen's heads whilst he stood behind them on the dais. Brenda had to smile when she saw how seriously he took his new task as squire to the Queens of Egypt and Sheba.

"That leaves you, dunnit?" The younger Queen of Egypt and Sheba sat up and peered at Brenda with interest. "Are you going to beg for mercy or what?"

Brenda looked at her defiantly. "You fed my friend to the crocodiles," she accused the queen. It wasn't quite true, for Lizzie had slipped back into the room adorned with feathers and armed with a spear, blending in with the other warriors.

"You! Squire," the younger queen turned to Eddie. "What shall we do to this traitor?"

"Feed to…," Eddie paused as he thought about his answer. "Feed her to spiders."

"Oh!" Brenda exclaimed. Eddie had picked the worst possible option, she hated spiders.

"Wait!" A new voice announced grandly. "I will vouch for this prisoner."

"HAIL MARC ANTHONY!" The warriors hollered dutifully as another boy came into the room, a bit shorter than Leon but equally attired in a makeshift toga and holly crown.

Marc Anthony came to stand next to Jules Ceasar. To her great surprise Brenda looked straight into the familiar bright blue eyes that belonged to Will Maskall.

Full scale Civil War broke out soon after that and the Royal Palace and surrounding area turned into a confusing battlefield. Eddie was delighted to be battling at Will's side again and the two ended as triumphant victors astride a heap of slain native American Egyptian legionnaires.

§ § § § § § §

Play came to an end and Brenda had wandered away from the palace with Will.

"I suppose you've found your adventures," Brenda said.

Will grinned. "It's not as bad as I thought but I still miss Brighton an awful lot."

"So do I," Brenda nodded wholeheartedly.

"The Hornsbys are fun though, aren't they?" Will smiled.

"I am not staying with them, they're our neighbours."

"Oh, who are you staying with then? Are they nice?"

"No, Will!" Brenda said. "They're horrible. It's all very well having fun and games but I've got to take Eddie back there afterwards, don't I?"

It came out more vehemently than Brenda intended, and she immediately regretted that for she could see that Will was taken aback.

"I'm sorry," she said quickly.

"Don't be," he answered. "I am sorry Brenda, when Lizzie told me you were staying at Hornsby Farm, I thought you were staying with her. You're mates, right?"

Brenda smiled. "Yes, Lizzie is my friend."

"I am glad you made a friend," Will said earnestly. "But the people you are staying with? How are they horrible?"

"They're stuck up," Brenda said. "Horribly posh and used to the luxury of proper town houses. They treat me like a servant! I spend every minute of the day washing and cooking and cleaning."

She continued her torrent of words for a while longer, it felt awfully good to be outside the Patterson sphere of influence and it felt good to be able to complain just for once. She could share a lot with Lizzie but was careful about mentioning the Pattersons because Brenda was afraid Lizzie might tell Mrs Hornsby, who might in turn try to talk to the Pattersons. Brenda didn't think talking to them would have much effect other than make things even more difficult.

Will listened to it all patiently and responded by shaking his head and tutting at all the right times.

"Goodness!" A terrifying thought struck Brenda. "Will, it's got late, I have to get back before they come home! We're not allowed to play in the woods!"

Lizzie came walking over. "Everything alright, Brenda?"

"Lizzie! I have to get back!" Brenda tried to insert urgency into her voice but it came out panicky. "Before they come back from church. We have to be there!"

"Don't worry about it," Lizzie assured her.

"But I have to! You don't understand!" Brenda was in a state of near-panic now. "They'll be ever so cross!"

Will gave her a troubled look.

"Easy, Brenda," Lizzie smiled. "My father will be waiting for us at Roreford, the ruins we passed, with the trap and all. He'll have you back in no time at all."

"He's waited all this time?" Brenda was astonished.

"He says that it's the only time of the week that he can relax in total peace. He'll be smoking his pipe and reading his papers," Lizzie grinned. "But to be sure, we can start walking back to Roreford now?"

Brenda nodded gratefully.

It took another ten minutes for the Hornsbys and their guests to say goodbye to everyone and Brenda was dizzied by the number of faces and names which passed her by in a rush. She noted that the Queens of Eqypt and Sheba were introduced as Joy and Maisy. Mostly she regretted that it was time to say goodbye to Will again.

"Are you going to be alright?" Will asked Brenda. She glanced at Lizzie.

"I'll Never Smile Again," Brenda said.

"Nobody Knows The Trouble I've Seen," Lizzie added.

"We'll Meet Again," Brenda promised Will.

"When The Saints Go Marching In," Lizzie added.

"And The Angels Sing," Brenda added.

"Over The Rainbow." Lizzie finished.

Will looked concerned.

"Never mind them," Leon told Will as he joined them. "There's naun sensible talk to be had when they're in this mood. Proper daft they are, tis unaccountable."

Will grinned. "Take care Brightonian."

"You too," Brenda left it at that. Although the day had been great fun and she regretted that it had to end, she was relieved nonetheless when the Hornsby troupe led her and Eddie to Roreford where Jasper Hornsby was indeed waiting. He loaded the two *Vackies* in his trap to speed them back towards the cottage.

When the Pattersons returned from church they found all the chores done and Brenda busily preparing the evening meal in the kitchen.

21. Moil in the Woods

Even without the complement of Hornsbys the Royal Palace was a scene of busy activity. A recent storm had knocked gaps in the roof and in other places the makeshift thatch was sagging down so there was plenty to do. Maisy had mobilised the entire Wolfden membership of the Wyrde Warriors. A greater part of the day was spent restoring the palace to royal splendour. When at last the work was done the Wyrde Warriors sank down to the ground and admired the result of their efforts.

"I don't mean to be immodest," Maisy announced grandly. "But we're blooming brilliant, ain't we?"

There were chuckles and murmurs of agreement.

Will looked at his cousin. The truth was that it had been Captain Robbins who had been brilliant. When they had arrived at the Royal Palace the visual impact of the damage had been disheartening. Even while the rest had stood there, their spirit as dishevelled as their HQ, Maisy had marched in, made a quick inspection, and walked out again with a mental list of required tasks and materials. She had ticked off work parties and then taken Major Maskall and Colonel-in-Chief Whitfield into the building for a more thorough inspection. Will and Joy had agreed with all of Maisy's suggestions. When the others came back with bracken, grass, and stout branches, new tasks were assigned and the work had progressed so rapidly to inject all with cheer. They had all been singing heartily before too long. Not the wireless stuff but the proper soldier songs; the ones that had originated in the trenches of the Great War.

Will had grinned at that. Half the parents of those present would have fainted if they heard the rough language, he suspected. The other half would be building a fence around the Wyrde Woods and declare it off-limits for the next century or so.

Maisy had been everywhere at once; encouraging, directing, correcting, praising, and chipping in where needed. Her presence had kept the momentum going.

Will had been observing the Wyrde Warriors with some thought since he had been recruited. Joy may have been the Colonel-in-Chief, but generally she hovered on the edges with a dreamy look on her face. Will had learned that could mean she was off in a world of her own or else just listening very carefully and keeping a sharp eye out on things. If and when Joy said anything everybody would listen though.

Maisy had spoken of the group's adventures plenty during the long walks from here to there and everywhere, so Will knew that the two girls had established their leadership in what sounded like genuine tests and obstacles before his arrival. Provided you were able to distil an interpretation from Maisy's stories, of course. That meant subtracting the divisions of Jerry spies, sinister castellans, squadrons of Amazons, as well as a plethora of native Pooks and scary ghosts. After that, Will reckoned, you'd arrive at something probably resembling what happened. Will was getting increasingly adept at following Maisy's erratic thoughts, sudden insights, impulsive ideas, and creative elaborations. She would still twist and turn too fast for him sometimes, but he was getting better at it. Jamie's conviction that all girls were silly, once shared by Will, would have been most seriously challenged by Maisy. Jamie had always been the more daring one who came up with the wilder plans but Maisy easily outshone Jamie in this.

As Captain of the Wyrde Warriors, Maisy was the engine that ran the whole operation. Like a people engineer, was Will's learned conclusion, though he was sure there was some proper posh word for it.

He was still trying to figure out his own role as Major. The other children respected him in the way they respected Leon; because he was one of the older boys in the group. Still, Will had kept to the background a little, resting on the laurels of his supposed combat experiences during the Brighton Blitz. That's how the rest saw it anyway, Will himself recalled his childish fury on his first outing in the Wyrde Woods and felt like a fake hero.

He had no idea how he would react again if…

§ § § § § § §

…the reason they had not immediately registered the approaching Heinkel He 111 bomber, all thirteen tons of the fully laden twin-engine bomber, was because its engines had not droned. Instead they had spluttered. When the stricken aeroplane came into sight, a little over one hundred and fifty feet overhead, it was spitting flame and smoke. The fifty-seven-foot-long fuselage and seventy-four-foot wingspan of the Heinkel impressed the children, all of whom were looking upward with their mouths hanging open. Usually the Heinkels showed as tiny crosses or glinting specks high up in the sky.

Even though it passed by in seconds, Will could see that it was on a steady trajectory of descent and in danger of making a roll and then corkscrewing into the ground. This plane was going to come crashing down sooner or later. Were the crew still on board?

Will jumped to his feet and shouted: "Armory! Get the bows and arrows! NOW!"

He began to run towards the Royal Palace. To his relief the others followed, making for the room where their weapons were stored. Will himself scrambled onto the roof as to be higher, in the vain hope of seeing more because a wider view was obstructed by the low treetops that surrounded the clearing. He heard rustling as Maisy and Joy came to join him.

"You think the crew jumped?" Maisy asked Will.

Will nodded. "Could be far off, but could be as near as the Roreford place, or Willikin's Drove."

"Could be right on top of us, ain't it?" Maisy suggested.

Will grinned at her ever-present urge to present the most cinematic scene she could think of.

"By Oak and Acorn!" Joy exclaimed in alarm.

Will's smile faded. Three men on parachutes came drifting into view. The wind was taking them straight to the clearing.

"Bloody Hell!" Maisy's eyes grew wide. "Jerry is coming, ain't he? About bloody time too."

22. Hell Hath no Fury

Brenda looked up in surprise when the Pattersons filed into the kitchen. They usually didn't come in until tea was ready. She was still in the midst of preparations while Eddie sat by the wireless, his ears close to the contraption because Children's Hour was on. Brenda had not heard the doors and had no chance to call out "Spitfire."

"Turn that infernal racket off, boy." Mr Patterson snapped at Eddie, who did as he was asked and then made himself as small as possible. Mrs and Mr Patterson seated themselves at the table.

"We need to talk, Brenda," Mrs Patterson said. "Sit down."

Brenda looked at them in disbelief, getting tea ready on time required careful timing and they themselves would be upset if it wasn't done properly.

"Yes ma'am," she said but first turned to attend her pans, placing them on the cooking range so that the soup and stew would not be burnt and caked to the bottom if left unstirred.

"This is precisely what the problem is," Mr Patterson complained. "The child ignores us, blatant disobedience. Sit down girl!"

The food was safe for the moment so Brenda wiped her hands on a tea towel and sat down nervously.

"We are not content," Mr Patterson told her.

"We have had to put up with considerable inconvenience already," Mrs Patterson told Brenda. "Taking the two of you in."

"Yes ma'am," Brenda said, looking down at the floor so they wouldn't see the flash of anger in her eyes.

"We received a letter from your school today," Mrs Patterson produced an envelope and brandished it in Brenda's face.

"Erm, school," Brenda mumbled. It was unlikely to be good news.

"Yes, school," Mrs Patterson said. "All we ask of you Brenda, is for a little consideration vis-à-vis our frail health."

"It's a matter of respect," Mr Patterson added.

"Receiving these types of letters, well it is not conducive to a weak constitution. Look at me when spoken to." Mrs Patterson said sharply.

Brenda looked up dutifully, though she desperately wanted to be elsewhere.

"The letter informs me that you have been handing in sloppy or incomplete assignments and falling asleep in class!" Mrs Patterson's voice became increasingly shrill as she listed Brenda's crimes. "FALLING ASLEEP IN CLASS, Brenda!"

"Education is wasted on the lower classes," Mr Patterson shook his head. "I've always said so."

Brenda bit on her lip at that remark because it was so unfair. She had never minded going to school and had always been eager to learn new things.

Gathering all her courage she said: "It's not fair."

"I will tell you what is not fair," Mrs Patterson said. "What is not fair is that we have been summoned to school to discuss your behaviour and the cause of it! You know we are poorly and should not undertake unnecessary journeys, Brenda. I am very disappointed in you."

"But you are the cause," Brenda blurted out.

"Excuse me?" Mrs Patterson's eyes bulged. "Are you blaming us now?"

"The ingratitude of it," Mr Patterson seemed incredulous.

Brenda looked at them with desperation. Mum had taught her not to talk back to adults, but Brenda did not see any other choice.

"With everything I have to do here in the house," she chose her words carefully, "I don't always have time to finish my schoolwork."

"Humbug," Mr Patterson said dismissively. "Time can be made for things which are truly important. You spend half-an-hour every evening reading fairy tales to your brother. You could have put that time to better use."

He peered at her over his spectacles and Brenda looked back helplessly.

"Eddie sleeps better if he's read to," she said softly.

"You pamper the child needlessly," Mr Patterson pronounced his judgement.

"I do a lot here; cooking, washing, cleaning!" Brenda insisted stubbornly.

"How much of this have you talked about at school?" Mrs Patterson demanded to know. "If you have been telling lies about us you will be in a world of trouble, young lady."

Mum. Dad. Help.

"Nothing!" Brenda cried. "I've told them that I was tired, that is all."

"You have some common sense then, which is a relief to know," Mr Patterson said.

"Nonetheless, they are bound to ask us as to the cause of this problem," Mrs Patterson tutted. "You will really have to try harder, Brenda."

"BUT I DO THE BEST I CAN!" Brenda shouted in frustration. She immediately covered her mouth with her hand. realising she had gone too far. Eddie uttered a soft whimper by the wireless.

"SILENCE!" Mr Patterson thundered. "Disobedience is a SIN."

"Dear Lord, you test us so," Mrs Patterson made a point of clutching her heart.

"It really is quite simple, girl," Mr Patterson said. "Perhaps it is hard to understand for you but there is a war on, you know, and we must all chip in and contribute. If you continue to be slack at school, I will find the time you need. Do not think I have not noticed that you devote considerable time to your brother?"

Brenda was numb and close to tears. She clenched her teeth and put on a brave face because she knew Eddie was watching her closely in order to make sense of the situation.

"We agreed to take him on but may have to revise that offer of generosity if he is too much of an obstruction to the efficiency of this household," Mr Patterson said.

Brenda's mouth dropped open, she could hardly belief what Mr Patterson was saying.

"It would yield you a great deal of extra time, we feel," Mrs Patterson added.

"Not Eddie," Brenda cried out, the tears beginning to escape from her eyes now. "You can't send Eddie away."

"Nooo!" Eddie wailed and hurled himself at Brenda, wrapping his arms around her and holding on to her tightly. "I want to stay with Brenda!"

Eddie began howling loudly, inconsolable now. Brenda turned to him to speak words of comfort, barely registering the shrill voices of the Pattersons demanding silence.

"SHUT THAT BOY UP!" Mr Patterson shrieked and rose to his feet.

Eddie stopped howling but his small body was racked by sobs and he snivelled too loudly as far as Mr Patterson was concerned.

"Very well," the man said and undid the buckle of his belt after which he pulled it out of the loops of his trousers.

"No, you can't!" Brenda cried.

"The boy needs a lesson," Mr Patterson said. "And you will stop talking back at me or you will get one too."

Eddie started howling again as Mr Patterson seized hold of him and tried to pry him loose from Brenda. The children struggled but then Mrs Patterson took hold of Brenda and pulled her away. Mr Patterson sat down on a chair and lifted Eddie over his knees. He raised the belt.

"Brenda!" Eddie wailed.

"Nooo!" Brenda twisted her body violently, tore herself loose from Mrs Patterson's clutches and rushed forward to place herself between that lifted hand and Eddie's bottom. She looked up at Mr Patterson's face in the hope of reasoning with him.

Mr Patterson struck but Brenda was in the way now and the belt impacted the side of her face with a loud crack. Stunned, Brenda fell to the ground and brought both her hands to the area of her upper cheek which stung ever so painfully. To her relief Mr Patterson let Eddie go and the boy flung his arms around Brenda's neck.

"I think it's time the both of you cooled off," Mrs Patterson said angrily. "Up, up on your feet."

When the children didn't respond she bent down and hooked her hands around their arms; clawing them tightly she pulled at them and Brenda and Eddie struggled to their feet.

After that Mrs Patterson steered them out of the kitchen and into the farmyard. She led them to a low pile of logs outside the woodshed and bade them sit down.

"You'll stay here and cool off, while we discuss what to do with you," Mrs Patterson ordered. "I suggest you reflect on your ingratitude."

"Ingratitude, ha," Brenda hissed.

"And your very improper manners," Mrs Patterson added. She turned around and went back into the cottage. Brenda experienced the temporary absence of Pattersons as a great relief rather than a punishment.

Eddie, sobbing softly, sought her arms and Brenda wrapped them around the boy while she took deep breaths to calm down because she was shaking and trembling like a leaf.

§ § § § § §

A cloud of misery enveloped Brenda even as she struggled not to succumb to it. She had so little though, to fight it with. Until now she had found straws of hope to clutch on to and kept herself as composed as possible for Eddie's sake, but she didn't know how long she could maintain that. Everything that had just happened marked a change, a point of no return. Whatever would be said during that meeting at school with the Pattersons didn't really even matter anymore. It was clear the Pattersons were not about to acknowledge the part they had played in Brenda's poor performance at school and would place all the blame squarely on Brenda's frail shoulders. If that meant Eddie would be taken away from her, to cope on his own, she would be hopelessly lost. How on earth would she tell Mum that she had failed to keep her promise.

"By Geemeny, lass," a woman's voice sounded; distant at first but when Brenda looked up, she could see that Jenny Hornsby had walked onto the farmyard and was approaching the woodpile Brenda and Eddie were huddled on. "'Tis far too cold for the two of you to be outside with no coats on."

Mrs Hornsby frowned. "I thought you would have had more sense than that, Brenda."

Brenda opened her mouth, then closed it again and just shook her head. The evening seemed to require an endless supply of explanations, all to be rent apart before she could even finish them. She had simply run out.

"Oak and Acorn! What's happened to your eye?" Mrs Hornsby asked. "Brenda?"

Brenda gingerly brought her fingertips to the place where Mr Patterson's belt had stuck her. The initial sharp stings had been reduced to a continuous throb that she had tried to ignore as best as she could. It was only now that she realised the force of impact had left a mark.

"'Tis all black and blued," Mrs Hornsby shook her head. "Has it been seen to?"

Brenda shook her head. "I took a fall, Mrs Hornsby."

"I don't believe a word of it, lass." Jenny Hornsby's face hardened. Brenda burst out into tears. Even though it was a fib there were only so many accusations she could handle.

"Mrs Hornsby." The cottage door opened and Mrs Patterson came out, warily approaching. "The children have punishment; they are not meant to be speaking to anybody."

Mrs Hornsby turned to face Mrs Patterson. She put her hands on her hips and planted her feet wide giving a clear message that she wasn't planning to budge.

Brenda paled. Things could only get worse this way. "Thank you for your concern, Mrs Hornsby," she said softly. "But it would really be best if you left now."

"You heard the girl, Mrs Hornsby," Mrs Patterson decreed. "These are private household matters. We are dealing with them."

Jenny Hornsby took a sharp intake of breath. "How did the lass get a black eye, Mrs Patterson? I care to know."

"It's my fault!" Eddie said.

"Your fault?" Jenny Hornsby looked at the boy with wonder.

"Children shouldn't speak when adults are talking," Mrs Patterson snapped at Eddie.

The boy cowered and threw Mrs Patterson a frightened look but then persisted. "The man want to hit me with his belt but Brenda got between."

"What is going on here?" Mr Patterson had come outside as well.

"You hit a child with a belt?" Jenny Hornsby's voice was very calm, but everybody could sense the latent anger beneath the surface.

"Children require correction, as I am sure you know," Mr Patterson said crisply. "If they are not to grow up feral and wild."

"Like countryside folk, you mean?" Jenny Hornsby challenged him. "I'll have you know that I've just about had enough of the two of you looking down at us as if you are the only ones who knows how disyer world works. All the time mistreating these poor chavees."

"All we ask is that they contribute to the…" Mrs Patterson protested.

"Contribute? Contribute?" Jenny Hornsby fumed, and Brenda held her breath. "You're letting disyer girl do all the work, from what I've seen and heard."

Mr Patterson gave Brenda a menacing look. "Heard?"

"We are poorly, struck down by our health…" Mrs Patterson began to say.

"OAKUM !" Jenny Hornsby thundered.

Both Pattersons took a startled backward step.

"Mrs Hornsby, I am sure we could discuss this matter…" Mr Patterson raised his hands palm up as if to ward off Jenny Hornsby's anger.

"Oh, we will," Jenny Hornsby said. "As soon as I've arranged for the Billeting Officer to visit us. In the meantime…" She turned to Brenda and Eddie. "I want you to go inside right now and pack your things. Bring them back outside please."

Brenda nodded and took Eddie's hand in her own. She made to step toward the front door.

"Don't you dare," Mr Patterson hissed at her. "You'd better call the many menfolk from your house here if you are going to force events in my household."

"The menfolk?" Jenny Hornsby spoke very softly. "Oh, naun, I will personally do to you what you did to this poor lass, I don't need the menfolk for that." She took a step forward and Brenda was amazed to see that Mr Patterson seemed to shrink with fear. He was afraid of Mrs Hornsby, she realised, though that was quite understandable because Lizzie's aunt was formidable in her anger. Brenda led Eddie inside and hastily gathered all their things together.

When they stepped out again the Pattersons were cowering in the face of a mighty tirade. Mrs Hornsby stopped mid-flow when she saw Brenda and Eddie come out.

"Come on chavees," she told them and turned around without a further word to the Pattersons. Brenda and Eddie followed her as she walked onto the road to the main farmhouse, evacuees once again, though this time they weren't wearing labels.

§ § § § § §

When Brenda and Lizzie walked out of school the next day, Eddie in tow, she was surprised to see Jeremy Hornsby waiting outside, atop the box of his wagon.

"How do?" He greeted them jovially.

"In need of a lift home, uncle Jer," Lizzie replied cheerfully.

"Thought so, hop in," Mr Hornsby replied.

"I didn't know you had to be in town today," Lizzie told him after the children had scrambled into the wagon.

Jeremy Hornsby turned around to face them and sighed.

"The Pattersons demanded I bring them to town. Even though I were right in the middle of work."

Brenda looked around in half a panic. Were they near to school?

"You should have told them…" Lizzie began to say.

"With their luggage and all, wanted to go to the station, so they did," Mr Hornsby winked at Brenda who suddenly held her breath. The farmer's face turned to one of utmost satisfaction when he added: "So I dropped all I was doing and said 'yes sir, yes ma'am' and brought them to the station as quick as I could. Made sure they got on that train too and waved them off."

"Good riddance!" Lizzie laughed.

"Do you mean…?" Brenda was puzzled.

Mr Hornsby changed his demeanour to one of earnesty.

"They have left the Wyrde Woods for good, Brenda, they shan't be coming back, and I for one, am glad to see the backs of them."

"They didn't even say goodbye?" Brenda asked, but then realised that she was pleased they hadn't. There was a much more pressing concern anyway. "But what are Eddie and I supposed to…"

"You'll be staying at the farmhouse with us, lass," Mr Hornsby said. "Until we get this sorted out."

"But…but…" Brenda stammered.

"My Jenny has decided, Brenda," Mr Hornsby grinned. "'Tis best not to argue with Goody Hornsby, it really bain't."

"Aunt Jen is the one in charge," Lizzie said happily.

Jeremy Hornsby nodded his agreement and turned to cluck at his horses. The wagon started rolling out of Odesby. Brenda looked at the passing scenery without really seeing any of it; there was too much to make sense of all at the same time and the only thing she knew for sure was that her ordeal seemed to have come to an end.

23. Local Heroes

"Form a line," Will shouted at the Wyrde Warriors who came rushing out of the Royal Palace. "There's no time to run," he told Maisy and Joy as all three of them scrambled down to take their place in the makeshift battle line.

To emphasize his words there was a light thud as the first airman made contact with the ground and started rolling over, straight into the folds of his parachute which had keeled over in front of him.

"Nock an arrow," Will called.

He pulled his catapult from his belt with one hand and took a marble from his ammo bag with the other. He did so without taking his eyes off the Germans. The two others landed now too. One with a shout of pain as he rolled over clutching his heel. The second made a perfect landing, looked to take in the scene at the thatched ruins, and then calmly undid his parachute harness.

"They've got pistols," Maisy hissed.

There was a tremendous explosion somewhere to the north. The Heinkel had crashed.

The archers around Will, Maisy, and Joy held their bows at the ready, the strings partially drawn.

The German airman who was on his feet drew a pistol from his holster. The first one who had landed was still shrouded below his parachute and they could see him wrestling with it. When he got himself disentangled he walked up to join the man with the drawn pistol. The other one was still moaning and clutching his ankle.

Maisy drew her cap gun and pointed it at them. "HANDS UP!"

The man with the drawn pistol laughed. "*Sie ist nur ein Kind mit einer Spielzeugpistole!*"

"*Genau, denk mal darüber nach, sie ist ein Kind mit einer Spielzeugpistole,*" the second one said.

"What are they talking about?" Will wondered out loud.

"I think they are discussing what to do with us," Joy said. "They are naun taking us very seriously, I reckon."

The airman with the gun laughed again and it made Will angry.

"DRAW!" He hollered. None of the children hesitated.

"Warning shot! Ten feet in front of target," Maisy added.

"LOOSE!" Joy called and a dozen arrows sped from the bows to thud into the ground in front of the airmen.

"NOCK A NEW ARROW!" Will shouted.

"*Gott im Himmel! Sie sind verrückt!*" The airman with the gun was astounded.

"*Hör auf!*" His companion shouted. "*Hör auf!* Stop it! All of you."

"SURRENDER!" Maisy shouted at him.

"Yes! Yes! We surrender!" The airman called back and then spoke urgently to the man with the pistol. "*Runter mit der Waffe.*"

"*Aber…*" the man answered.

"*Unser Kampf ist vorbei. Waffe auf den Boden. JETZT!!*"

To Will's relief the man with the pistol laid it on the ground and reluctantly raised his arms into the air.

"We are taking our guns out of our holsters one by one. Yes?" The airman who had taken charge shouted.

"PUT THEM ON THE GROUND." Maisy called at them.

"*Das ist gut!* That is good!" The man answered her and then told the other airmen. "*Nimm die Patronen raus.*"

The archers shifted about nervously, their bows were up and at half-draw again. As soon as Will saw that the Germans were taking the ammo out of the guns and discarding them, he ordered: "STAND DOWN!"

Everybody seemed to sigh a very deep breath of relief when the two Germans who could walk came forwards slowly with their hands raised in the air.

"Children!" The leader called out and grinned. "You are crazy children, yes?"

"Blimey yes, we're daft as hell but cracking," Maisy confirmed.

The Colonel-in-Chief, Major, and Captain held a quick consultation.

"I'd like to have one of them pistols, don't I?" Maisy threw a longing look at the discarded guns.

"So would I," Will said. "For my collection."

"Gramps will never let us have them," Maisy shrugged. "We'd best collect them in a sack, ain't it?"

"Take them to the Raven's Roost?" Joy asked.

Maisy nodded. Then her eyes sparkled. "Get them parachutes though, fold them up, hide them somewhere dry."

Will grinned. "I'll see to it."

§ § § § § §

"WHAT THE PIZE ARE YOU TWO UP TO NOW?" Fred Maskall's eyes glinted dangerously.

He had met them on the long dirt road which led from Roreford to the Raven's Roost. He was leading a complement of Home Guard soldiers looking for the downed aircrew. They had seen the plane and parachutes, and now stared at the children who proudly surrounded their three prisoners of war. The Germans looked harmless because the two who could walk carried their injured comrade between them, his arms around their shoulders as he hopped on one leg.

"They dropped right on top of us, Grip," Maisy said, using her special nickname for Gruncle Maskall. "Came down from a crippled Heinkel, didn't they?"

"It's true, Gruncle," Will added. "We were at our fort."

"There was no time to run, Mus Maskall," Joy added.

Gruncle Maskall shook his head and looked from his wayward charges to the prisoners.

"Did you disarm them?"

"Yes Grip, and they took the bullets out," Maisy reluctantly handed him a jute sack. Gruncle Maskall took it and glanced inside.

"Well," he shook his head again and then looked at the airmen. Their leader saluted him with his free hand.

"*Oberleutnant* Schmitt," he said. "*Luftwaffe*. I have surrendered to Captain Robbins, we will cause no trouble, yes?"

"Sergeant Maskall," Will's gruncle answered. "Home Guard. You will behave?"

"My war is over now, Sergeant," Schmitt shrugged. "I do not fight children."

HOW ABOUT THE ODEON?! Will wanted to protest but he kept his mouth shut.

"Thank you, *Oberleutnant* Schmitt," Gruncle Maskall said, "I will have to have you frisked." He signalled and three of his men came forwards to pat down the German airmen.

Gruncle Maskall turned to the children again when no weapons were found. "Tis unaccountable, lead on your prisoners then, we'll fall in step."

Will was pleased that Gruncle Maskall let the children lead the captives, although he noticed that his gruncle's men took position all around them and had their rifles at the ready.

"The two of you are scaddles," Gruncle Maskall told Will and Maisy as the procession moved on again.

"Yes, Gruncle," Will admitted.

"Yes, Gramps," Maisy said.

"If there's any hurley-bulloo to be found you two are in the midst of it. You too Joy Whitfield. I ought to give all three of you a right bannicking."

"Yes, Grip."

"Yes, Gruncle."

"Aye, Mus Maskall."

All three grinned as they answered.

"Don't think Sarah would object, Joy Whitfield, you are warned."

"You're the only one she'd accept it from, Mus Maskall," Joy acknowledged.

"Nought but grout-headed puck-stooled rogues," Gruncle Maskall complained. "My Betty is gwoan skin you all alive, mark my words. Taking on Jerry sodgers, tis middling unaccountable, sureleye."

"Yes, Gruncle."

"Aye, Mus Maskal."

"Yes, Grip."

§ § § § § §

There was quite a reception at the Raven's Roost. Home Guard soldiers were milling about, there were two lorries from the Canadian base at Mordrove, and Canadian soldiers too. Even a newspaper reporter and a photographer.

When the Wyrde Warriors and their captives and Home Guard escort emerged from the footpath at the crossing, the soldiers formed a curious circle. A Canadian officer and the commander of the Wolfden Home Guard stepped forward.

"What is the meaning of this?" The Home Guard officer said in a loud voice. He looked at Gruncle Maskall, "Sergeant Maskall, report."

"Bain't my circus," Gruncle Maskall said softly. "Gwoan, claim your glory."

"Colonel-in-Chief?" Maisy asked Joy, but Joy shook her head.

"Go on, Maise," Will said when she looked at him. Maisy grinned and marched forward. When she came to the two officers, she stamped a foot on the ground, stood straight, and executed a perfect salute like a miniature soldier.

"Captain Robbins, Special Detachment, Royal Sussex Regiment!" She announced loudly.

The officers looked her up and down, and then stood at attention to return her salute.

Will could only see Maisy's back from where he stood but he had no doubt that she was grinning from ear to ear and bursting with pride. He and Joy were too, and even Gruncle Maskall seemed to be regarding them all with proud pleasure on his face.

LOCAL HEROES

ODESB)
BOMB
DAMAG

William Maskall (13) and Maisy Robbins (11) of Maskall Farm on North Woods Lane and Joy Whitfield (12) of the Owlery became local Wolfden heroes last Saturday. Lt. Mackellow, commander of the local Home Guard was delighted when the

The recent Luftwaffe a on Odesby was conducte two Heinkel HE bombers, the Chief Wa of the Odesby ARP has The intended target n have been the indus estate north of the rai station rather than Neverland residential e which bore the brunt of attack. Then again it been suggested the attac a civilian target may have been planned in attempt to take the figh spirit out of the popula There was no such fea

24. The Season to be Jolly

Brenda quickly discovered that being abandoned by the Pattersons was close to a miracle. The Hornsby men spent an hour in the great big loft dormitory where the Hornsby children slept and in that space of time managed to add the extra beds, bedside tables, and closets into the loft to meet the needs of the new full complement of eight children.

"You'll have to move back to the cottage, Brenda," Mrs Hornsby told the girl. "When it's assigned new occupants. Howsumdever, until then we're naun gwoan leave you there all by yourself."

"Thank you, Mrs Hornsby," Brenda said, hiding her disappointment.

Mrs Hornsby smiled. "Try naun to be afeared, lass. I've let the committee know all about the Pattersons and have been assured they'll take the mix with chavees into better consideration."

Brenda nodded although she didn't look forward to assimilate into a whole new situation once again. Fortunately, assimilation into the Hornsby household, chaotic as it was, was smooth beyond belief. There were chores, more so even because the Hornsbys ran a working farm, but the Hornsby children threw themselves at most tasks with determined enthusiasm and many hands made light work.

Brenda was delighted to find herself freed from the burden of being the sole person in charge of her brother. Eddie merged in with the two youngest Hornsbys without a hitch and their care was a collective task at the Hornsby household. Whenever it occurred to Brenda that Eddie needed to wash his hands, brush his teeth, or put on his pajamas, she would find that Mrs Hornsby, Lizzie, Leon, or even the adult men were already herding the youngest three this way or that to get things done.

Whether or not it was expected Brenda didn't know but she often found herself helping Lizzie in Mrs Hornsby's kitchen. Feeding the large family was a full-time job and Brenda greatly enjoyed pitching in. Not only was she aware that she and Eddie were two extra mouths to feed and therefore more work, but the kitchen was a fun place to be. Mrs Hornsby ran a tight ship and never asked Lizzie or Brenda to take on more than they could handle. She kept a sharp eye on things but never ceased to produce good-natured chatter.

"Good job, bettermost done," she complimented Brenda one day and Brenda smiled.

"Now, I need you both to come out with me," Mrs Hornsby told Brenda and Lizzie. "The menfolk have plowed my onion field."

The onion 'field' was a large corner of a paddock which had been added to Mrs Hornsby's vegetable patch to supplement rations and produce extra vegetables for the market in Odesby. Mrs Hornsby led the two girls to the corner of the onion field and produced two hazel shoots which Brenda had seen her cut in the small hazel copse behind the haystacks earlier.

"Lizzie, will you show Brenda how tis done?" Mrs Hornsby handed one of the hazel rods to Lizzie.

Lizzie's face grew solemn and she flattened a patch of ploughed earth in the very corner with her foot. Then she drew a heart flanked by two crosses in the earth.

"Can you remember that, Brenda?" Mrs Hornsby asked.

"Yes, Mrs Horsnby." Brenda nodded.

"Good lass." Mrs Hornsby handed over the other hazel rod. "Lizzie, you take the far corner if you please. Brenda, I'd be much obliged if you could draw this sign in the two remaining corners."

Brenda was puzzled but did as she was asked and tried to imitate the solemnity she had seen on Lizzie's face; this was clearly an important moment. She took care in drawing the heart and crosses twice and then returned to Mrs Hornsby to give back the hazel shoot just as Lizzie had done.

Mrs Hornsby held both shoots up. "We shall burn these in the fire tonight to seal the charm."

"Charm?" Brenda asked. 'Curiouser and curiouser' Alice had said in Wonderland and this was how she must have felt at times, Brenda reckoned.

"Aye." Mrs Hornsby smiled. "A garden blessed by a child is safe from the Farisees, and you have just blessed my onion field, Brenda."

"Farisees?" Brenda asked.

"Pooks," Lizzie explained.

Brenda smiled back. She thought it an odd little custom, but Mrs Hornsby seemed very pleased and Brenda was glad that she had played a part in that.

Brenda helped clear the table after tea and the hours after that could be spent any way she pleased. The Hornsby men would sit by the open fire and read newspapers or smoke a pipe whilst the children concentrated around the table to read a book, play a game, or frown at their homework.

Brenda and Lizzie helped the three youngest children fabricate Christmas decorations this evening. This mostly involved cutting coloured paper into strips and gumming the interlocking loops to make garlands, but Brenda and Lizzie also used old wallpaper to cut and paste angels to hang in the tree. The girls loved doing that and competed in making ever more complex patterns, to the acclaim of the three youngsters.

The Christmas preparations continued during Brenda's second wonderful week in the Hornsby household. She and Lizzie accompanied Leon and the men into the Wyrde Woods to gather real holly with pretty red berries while they dug out a four-foot-high fir tree. The holly and garlands were used to decorate the front room and Leon helped his father place the tree in a decorated bucket filled with wet mud.

"Naun need to kill it," Jeremy Hornsby grumbled. Then the children were allowed to festoon the tree with their homemade decorations. Goody Hornsby provided a roll of cotton from which Brenda and Lizzie plucked balls to make snow or rolled threads to hang their angels up with. A box of battered candle holders was produced. Goody Hornsby attached these to the twigs and inserted little red candles.

Brenda thought the Christmas Tree turned out splendid and would often open the door and peek into the front room to admire it. Will Maskall visited with his great uncle, in a small farm wagon which transported a treasure. Will's great uncle traded a ham and several rabbits for some Hornsby cider and a bottle of home-brewed cider brandy, and everybody was content with the deal. Tea and sugar rations had been increased in the week before Christmas but not so ham, bacon, and butter so some improvisation was called for.

Brenda spent some time talking to Will but then Eddie began tugging at Will's hand. Her brother wanted to show Will his 'Secret Time' places around the Hornsby land and do so all on his own. Brenda watched the two walk off. Will had grown taller and Eddie dribbled furiously to ensure that he set the pace, not the older boy. He was chatting Will's ears off, probably about Tigger, Buntings, and Pooh, but Will seemed to like the esteem Eddie held him in so Brenda knew they were both happy.

As Christmas came ever closer Brenda began to fervently hope that the new occupants of the cottage wouldn't arrive until after the holiday because she was really looking forward to spending Christmas at the

Hornsbys. These hopes were dashed by the local billeting officer though. When Brenda spotted the silver-haired woman from Odesby driving her car up the Hornsby Farm access road she felt shivers all over and struggled to maintain her self-control as she went inside the kitchen to tell Mrs Hornsby that a visitor was about to arrive.

Mrs Hornsby wiped her hands on her apron and then washed them as she instructed Lizzie to welcome the visitor and usher her into the front room.

Brenda helped Lizzie prepare a fresh pot of tea and followed her friend to the frontroom to open the door for her as Lizzie carried the pot, cream, precious sugar, and cups on a tray.

"So, we don't know yet," Brenda heard the local billeting officer say. "Possibly Christmas Eve but it could be Christmas Day or Boxing Day."

"We'll have the cottage ready," Mrs Hornsby replied.

Brenda's heart sank as she pushed the door open fully so that Lizzie could enter. It seemed as if her Christmas hopes would be dashed and Brenda dearly wanted to cry.

Lizzie made it better when she came out of the front room again.

"I'm Sending A Letter To Santa Claus," she told Brenda.

"I've Got A Pocketful of Dreams," Brenda replied.

"They Can't Take That Away From Me," Lizzie said.

"Never In A Million Years," Brenda said fervently and they left it at that.

25. Christmas Morning

Will and Maisy bounded down the stairs in the morning, far wider awake than they were any other morning of the year. Spilling into the living room they immediately spotted the array of coloured packages beneath the Christmas tree. Whooping wildly, they made to charge the tree but Granny Maskall, up and about already, put a stop to that.

"Your gaffer is out milking," she shouted from the kitchen. "We'll wait until he gets back and share a cup of tea first. You can unwrap your presents afterwards."

Will and Maisy nodded at each other. The odds of surviving that long a wait were terrible, but it only seemed fair that Fred Maskall would be present. Will started circling the tree, stalking to and fro as he mentally catalogued the presents but then Maisy took his hand and pulled him out of the living room and into the kitchen.

Maisy walked towards Granny Maskall and wrapped her arms around her grandmother.

"Merry Christmas, Gran!"

"Oh, dear me," Granny Maskall laid her hand on Maisy's head. "Merry Christmas Maisy, Merry Christmas Will."

Will smiled at his great aunt. "Merry Christmas Granny."

Gruncle Maskall entered the kitchen, closing the door quickly because of the cold and then taking off his scarf and farmyard coat. There was another round of 'Merry Christmas' before they settled down around the table for a cup of tea.

"We'll have to do the presents afore breakfast, Fred," Granny Maskall said. "There's naun reason to make the chavees suffer anymore than they already are, sureleye." She indicated Will and Maisy who were doing their best to look angelic but unable to sit still; squirming on their chairs and fidgeting with everything in reach of their hands.

"Oh, but I like to have breakfast first, so I do," Gruncle Maskall answered. He chuckled at Will and Maisy's crestfallen expressions. "We could tie the chavees up? I could fetch some rope."

"I'll help you tie up Will." Maisy brightened. "We could hang him from the hooks in the chimney with the hams and smoke him, couldn't we?"

"No, we'll cram you into the oven first," Will replied.

"That's the Christmas spirit," Gruncle Maskall beamed.

Granny Maskall tutted. "I don't know which of you three is the worst, tis unaccountable. Mayhap, naun of you deserve a gift."

"We love each other, really!" Maisy interjected. "Don't we, sweet cousin?"

"Yes, we do!" Will nodded. "My dearest cousin is absolutely right."

220

"By Geemeny." Gruncle Maskall shook his head. "If I were a suspicious man, I would suggest these two chavees are conning us, Betty. To make us believe they are bettermost chavees."

"We are!" Maisy nodded. "Finest chavvies in all of England, Guv."

"I suppose we could have our cuppa in the…" Fred Maskall began to say but Will and Maisy cheered before he could finish.

"Careful with your mugs," Betty Maskall said. "Wait, why don't I carry them in on a tray?"

The two elder Maskalls seemed to take forever to cross to the living room where Will and Maisy had seated themselves on the floor, lively with anticipation.

There were several small packages for Will and Maisy which contained a selection of sweets. The elder Maskalls both got a book; Graham Greene's latest novel *The Power and the Glory* for Fred Maskall and Agatha Christie's recently published *Sad Cypress* for Betty Maskall. The larger packages contained jumpers which Granny Maskall had knitted for Will and Maisy and they immediately pulled them on.

That left two very small wrapped packages under the tree which the children eyed curiously. The smallest one was for Maisy. She removed the wrapping paper slowly and carefully so that it could be used again. Inside was a small flat cardboard box. Maisy gasped when she opened it. Will craned his neck to see. There was a small shiny locket on a chain, the whole sparkling brightly. It must have cost a pretty penny and Maisy looked at Granny Maskall with an open mouth, still not daring to take the locket out of the box.

"You'll be twelve soon, Maisy," Granny Maskall said. "A young lady should have some jewellery."

"It's beautiful, ain't it?" Maisy gingerly lifted the locket from the box. She discovered a minute lock and pressed it so that the locket sprung open to reveal portraits of her mother and father. Will smiled when he saw Maisy's eyes grow moist. Maisy closed the locket again and walked to Granny Maskall.

"Can you put it on for me?"

Granny Maskall obliged and fastened the chain around Maisy's neck. Maisy pressed her chin against her chest so she could admire the locket, then she looked at Will and Gruncle Maskall.

"How do I look?" She demanded to know.

"You are the fairest one of all," Gruncle Maskall smiled.

"You look very pretty, Maise," Will said.

Maisy beamed and sat down.

"NEXT!" She hollered with a foolish grin and then pressed her chin down again to look at the locket.

"Wait," Will said, looking awkward. "There's this too, Maisy." He produced a flat rectangular carton box and thrust it at his cousin.

"Huh?" Maisy's face fell. "Will, I didn't get you…"

"That's alright, just unwrap it." Will was eager to see Maisy's reaction.

"Cor blimey!" Maisy exclaimed when she opened the lid of the box.

"What is it Maisy-mine?" Gruncle Maskall asked.

"The Western Desert Force really gave the Italians a bloody nose in Egypt, didn't they?" Maisy said enthusiastically.

"It's the newspaper the present is wrapped in, Gruncle," Will said. "Open the newspaper you silly duck."

"Alright, Brighton Blighter," Maisy lifted the newspaper. "Patience is a virtue, ain't it? And you ha…"

Maisy's voice died into nothingness. Will grinned.

"By Geemeny," Granny Maskall shook her head. "The lad's got Maisy speechless. Tis unaccountable."

Gruncle Maskall agreed, "Tis a Christmas miracle, sureleye."

Maisy retrieved a sturdy hawthorn catapult from the newspaper wrapping and held it up; her mouth still wide open.

"I've got Jamie's Spitfire," Will said. "And the blackthorn catapult his dad made me. You should have this."

"Blimey! Will! I can't!" Maisy turned her hand so that Jamie's catapult lay on her palm.

"I want you to have it," Will said and folded Maisy's hand over the catapult. He added in a very soft voice: "It's important to me."

Will gave her a pleading look; hoping she wouldn't make him go all soppy. Maisy understood and nodded with a grateful smile.

"Well, if I'd be doing you a favour…" she started.

Gruncle Maskall laughed. "Will's turn, the last gift."

Will retrieved it from underneath the tree. He unwrapped it carefully and was puzzled to discover a short small paint brush and a little pot of white gloss paint. He gave Gruncle Maskall an enquiring look.

"Your present bain't complete, Will," Fred Maskall said slowly, savouring his words.

Will grinned uncertainly; he had more or less expected that to be the case, but it didn't answer his unspoken question.

"You'll need your Tommy helmet, Will." Granny Maskall smiled mysteriously.

"My helmet?" Will asked.

"To paint a big white 'M' on it," Gruncle Maskall explained.

A white 'M'. That was what ARP messenger boys had on their helmets. Will shook his head. "But I ain't fourteen yet."

"Well, a certain Home Guard Sergeant has vouched that you are, and his words carry some weight in Wolfden," Granny Maskall's eyes sparkled with mischief.

"But…but…you need a bicycle," Will said slowly.

Fred Maskall grinned at him and Will felt his heart skip a beat. Granny Maskall started grinning too and then Maisy laughed.

"They're a bit slow on the uptake in Brighton, ain't it? Not like London chavvies," she said. "I'll help you look for it, Will. I betcha it's hidden on the farm somewhere."

Will nodded, staring at the elder Maskalls with incredulity, hardly daring to believe it.

"Well, come on then!" Maisy jumped up.

"Coats, scarves, mittens and headwear," Granny Maskall ordered.

"We won't be long," Maisy objected.

"Oh, I think you'll find it is lamentably well hidden," Gruncle Maskall grinned. "I suspect you'll be out there for a while."

He winked at Granny Maskall. Will laughed and jumped up to race Maisy to the kitchen where they hurried into their winter gear before rushing outside to turn the farm upside down to look for Will's bicycle.

26. The Best Gift of All

Christmas morning at the Hornsbys was everything Brenda had hoped it would be. She had spent most of the day before Christmas consumed by the dreadful fear that the cottage's new occupants would turn up, but to her relief the access road had remained empty all day. A rowdy and noisy breakfast was eaten before three adults and eight children crowded into the front room to light a fire in the hearth, light the candles in the tree, and start unpacking the gifts piled beneath the tree.

All the children received a pack of sweets which Brenda and Lizzie had helped Mrs Hornsby make earlier that week and the Hornsby children received various items of knitted clothing. The men had been busy with their carving knives and there were untold homemade toys to be unwrapped, including a doll's house for the younger girls, intricate farm wagons with horses for the younger boys, and even a set of brightly painted coloured blocks for Eddie who was much enamoured with his gift. Lizzie and Brenda both got a set of colour pencils and drawing paper and Brenda felt overwhelmed by the generosity.

When all the gifts had been unwrapped and everybody had settled down to admire them, Brenda and Lizzie withdrew into a corner to draw the Christmas tree with the many wall-paper angels which hung in it. The wireless had been brought in from the kitchen and turned on and the room seemed bright with carols and laughter.

After about an hour Brenda and Lizzie left the room with Mrs Hornsby to help prepare the Christmas lunch.

"Could you set the table for thirteen please," Mrs Hornsby asked Brenda who was mightily puzzled by the request. Adding up all the grown-ups and children in the house told her what she had realised immediately; the Hornsbys were expecting two more guests.

Brenda set the table but her good cheer was gone, and she felt as if a ball of tension was contracting in her tummy. She had steeled herself to the inevitable new occupancy of the cottage and the long process of getting used to new adult faces and peculiarities but had finally dared to hope it wouldn't be until after Christmas. The prospect of spending most of the rest of the day in the cottage in the presence of strangers would be a cold shower contrasted to the warmth of the Hornsby household on this special day.

Mrs Hornsby was as busy as a bee but kept an eye out on the farmyard through the windows. Brenda's heart sank when she nodded and said: "Lizzie, mind the kitchen please. Brenda, could I speak to you outside for a moment?"

Brenda nodded and followed Mrs Hornsby through the door to step into the farmyard.

Mrs Hornsby laid both her hands on Brenda's shoulders and gave her a kind smile.

"Don't look so worried lass," she said. "Everything will be fine."

"I am worried though," Brenda protested. "And nobody has told me anything, I don't know what is going on."

Brenda startled herself with the outburst; it was bad manners but Mrs Hornsby just gave her another smile in response.

"There were too many uncertainties, sweetie," she said. "But that's over now."

She glanced down the access road and Brenda followed her look. A light trap had diverted from the main road and was making its way toward Hornsby farm. Brenda could just make out that there were two passengers behind the driver. She looked up at the grey forbidding sky to force back the moisture which was welling up behind her eyes.

"Now there is something I must tell you," Mrs Hornsby's voice drew Brenda's eyes back to her host. "I don't want you to be alarmed, lass. Nobody was hurt."

Brenda's eyes grew wide.

"I am afraid your home in Brighton has been bombed," Mrs Hornsby said. "Your mum and dad were both at work, but I understand it was a direct hit and there wasn't much left of the house."

Brenda swallowed and nodded. Poor mum and dad. To be made homeless at this time of year was awful. Then it struck her that she would never see her home again because it was all gone and she felt dizzy.

The kitchen door opened. Leon stepped outside, leading Eddie by the hand.

"There you are," Eddie said. "Do you want to play blocks?"

Brenda smiled at her little brother, innocently shielded from the horrible knowledge that she was still trying to digest.

"They're not homeless, sweetie," Mrs Hornsby told Brenda. "Skilled labourers and nurses are in great demand and a transfer has been arranged. I didn't tell you before because we weren't sure yet."

Brenda nodded mutely. It made sense but somewhere inside of her she felt a spark of anger that Christmas morning had been chosen to impart the terrible news from Brighton. It would have been far kinder to be kept in the dark for one more day.

"Mummy and Daddy," Eddie tugged at Brenda's sleeve.

"Yes Eddie," Brenda forced a smile. "We're talking about them."

"No Brenda," Eddie tugged her sleeve again. "You don't understand."

"Eddie please, I am talking to Mrs Hornsby," Brenda tugged her sleeve loose from the boy's grip, suddenly feeling the burden of her responsibility for the boy again.

"No Brenda!" Eddie insisted. "Look! Look! Mummy and Daddy!"

Her brother pointed at the access road on which the trap had come near enough to identify the faces of the man and woman seated in the back. Brenda's mouth dropped open.

She turned to look at Mrs Hornsby who bestowed another smile on her.

"I asked Lady Priscilla from Malheur Hall for help," Mrs Hornsby told Brenda. "The Malheurs own a few factories and there is a surgery in Odesby in need of a new nurse. They've come to stay, sweetie."

Brenda shook her head in disbelief.

"Well, gwoan then, lass," Mrs Hornsby said. "Tell them Christmas lunch is nearly ready and they're most welcome on Hornsby Farm. And Rodmelle Cottage."

Eddie grabbed her hand and squeezed it and she squeezed back, after which the two children ran across the farmyard hand-in-hand to greet their parents. So far Christmas in the Weald had exceeded all of Brenda's expectations, but this was surely the best gift of all.

27. 'M'

Will stood in the farmyard, his bicycle by his side. He wore a blue coverall with a red embroidered ARP badge on it. There was also a brand-new shiny ARP pin on his lapel. His battered and faded Tommy helmet sported a bright white 'M'. The bicycle was an old one but Gruncle Maskall had taken it apart and rebuilt it in his workshed so that nothing rattled, the brakes worked, and it too had a new coat of paint.

Gruncle Maskall and Granny Maskall stood in front of Will. There was no sign of Maisy and Will was a little disappointed that she had not come to see him off.

"I've made you some extra sandwiches; Maskall ham and mustard." Granny Maskall had packed the sandwiches in paper and gave these to Will who took them gratefully.

"Thank you, Granny," he smiled.

"Goodness knows when you'll be fed at the Raven's Roost," she said, referring to the pub outside of Wolfden where all Wolfden's civil defence efforts were co-ordinated.

"Oakum," Gruncle Maskall said. "There'll be hot tea and sandwiches for the lad. The same grub I get, though, naun as good as yours, my nightingale, that much is true." He looked Will up and down and Will straightened his back.

"Do you, William Maskall," his great uncle looked Will into the eye. "Understand that this bain't a game?"

Will nodded. This would be an adventure of different sorts.

"You might be back tonight, or tomorrow, or not until Sunday," Gruncle Maskall continued. "I don't know the roster for the ARP staff. I got you in, but I cannot interfere with their business at the Raven's Roost."

Will nodded, he didn't want that kind of special treatment anyway. "I'll do as I am told."

"Your schoolwork must naun suffer all-along-of it," Gruncle Maskall warned. "You'll take it with you if you have duty on school nights."

"And when you are here," Granny Maskall added. "There'll still be chores on the farm."

Will nodded again. He would certainly be kept occupied.

"Well," Gruncle Maskall said, "I'm on duty tomorrow, so I will probably see you there. We may be allowed to share a cup of tea."

"Yes, Sergeant Maskall," Will grinned.

"You look the part," Gruncle Maskall ended his goodbye. "Wilfred and George would have been proud of you, lad."

Will felt his chest swell with pride.

"Thank you, thank you both, for everything."

"Off you go then, we've got work to do," Granny Maskall tutted. "You're keeping us from our tasks."

Will grinned one last time and then swung his leg over the back of the bicycle, took place on the saddle, and used his legs to push the bike into motion. His feet caught the pedals and he started pushing them down and around and then cycled down the access lane towards the North Woods Lane where he took a left turn.

Will had been a mediocre cyclist the week before his Christmas gift but he had spent every free second he could find to practise and as a result he felt comfortable with the bicycle, it had already become an extension of him. Though part of him felt as if he was embarking on a grand adventure there was an overriding sense that he would cross a threshold when he walked into the Raven's Roost to report for duty. No longer would he be a victim of the war, pushed around by circumstances. Instead, he would do his bit to fight back, play a part in the war at last, and assume the responsibilities of a man.

About halfway to the Raven's Roost, Will became aware of the rapid thuds of hoofbeats behind him. He turned to look but before he had even caught a glimpse of the approaching rider he looked forward again as his movement had unbalanced him and the bicycle had started to swerve. The identity of the rider rapidly became clear anyhow.

"HEEEEEEHAW!!!" Maisy hollered as she galloped past on her pony Spark. "MAKE WAY FOR THE WOLFDEN PONY EXPRESS!"

"Maisy!" Will protested but Maisy thundered on towards the Raven's Roost.

"I'll race you!" She shouted and waved her hat in the air and whooped.

Will pedalled harder in pursuit but Maisy and Spark were winning distance rapidly. He saw them again when he arrived at the Raven's Roost. Sparks was drinking water from a trough. Maisy was chatting to one of the Home Guard soldiers who stood near her. To Will's surprise Joy was there as well. Then he recalled that Maisy was to spend her weekend at the Owlery, they must have agreed to meet at the Raven's Roost.

"So, you see, Private Rye," Maisy suddenly increased her volume when she spotted Will hopping off his bike. "I've come to pass the message that a messenger boy is approaching, possibly with a message, ain't it? Of course, you would have known faster if you made use of the new Wolfden Pony Express service. 'The mail must go through' is our motto."

"That's middling clever of you, Captain Robbins," the soldier said to Maisy and grinned at Will.

"I won the race Will, Londoners are fast, ain't we?" Maisy told her cousin.

"Very funny," Will said. "I haven't got time to play, I've come for my orders."

"Will?" Maisy tilted her head at him and smiled. "Best of luck. Make me proud."

"Thanks, Maise." Will smiled back. "I shall."

Then Joy stepped forwards. "Good luck sodger boy."

"Tha…" Will began to say but Joy shut him up by stepping forwards and planting a kiss on his cheek.

"EWW!!!" Maisy called out. "That's disgusting!"

Joy stepped back again, looking smugly at Will who had turned bright red and was opening and closing his mouth like a landed fish.

"You're still a scaddle, Will Maskall," Joy said.

"Duck," Will found his breath again. Then he looked at the main entrance of the Raven's Roost and marched towards it resolutely, half floating on the air because of that kiss. He decided that girls were silly when you were twelve, but less so when you were thirteen and nearly grown-up. Jamie would be twelve forever so it would be up to Will to discover these things on his own from now on. Nonetheless, Jamie would have been bloody proud of his best mate, about to report for duty in a proper uniform, cheek still tingling from a pretty girl's kiss. War had brought Will Maskall many changes. Not all of them were pleasant but this was certainly a bright moment. The future was uncertain, and nobody knew what it would bring. Will might lose himself yet, but at this particular moment all was well in Will's War.

THE END

Acknowledgements

As always there are a number of people without whom this book couldn't have been written. First and foremost, I must thank Bren Hall, not only for her editing work (together with Lesley Bourke), but also for the many hours of research into evacuee experiences in wartime Sussex. This allowed me to plough on with the narrative, rapidly supplied with the background information I needed.

I also owe a great deal to Tommy Tickle (Clown on a Moped) for his generosity and hospitality. Liesel Lehrhaupt provided the usual narrative brainstorming assistance, and Benjamin Tritschler was very forthcoming in correcting my poor German. Kayleih Kempers provided another brilliant illustration, as well as the two older ones I included in this book. Julie Gorringe did a remake of the cover that I personally think is fantastic, so many thanks are due there too. Special mention to Gerrit Orgers for exploring Brighton with me, culminating in a memorable catapult shoot at Banjo Groyne in honour of Will and Jamie. Many thanks as well to Gerrit's daughters Anna and Rozemarijn who provided so much of Joy and Maisy's characters, and who feature on the cover of this book. Last-but-not-least, Janet and Cair Going for proofreading and cheerleading.

Will's War in Exile ends the historical Will's War series, but Will Maskall will continue to play a part in the expanding saga of the Wyrde Woods, along with Maisy and Joy.

Nils Nisse Visser, Brighton, April 2016 & October 2020.
www.nilsnissevisser.co.uk

More adventures of Will, Maisy & Joy can be found in:

Will's War in Brighton
(Historical wartime fiction, summer 1940)

War has brought many changes to Will Maskall's Brighton. It all seems like a grand adventure at first, but Will, his best friend Jamie, and Jamie's neighbour Brenda soon discover the darker side of growing up in a war-torn town. Although fiction, many of their adventures are based on the recollections and anecdotes of Brightonians who were children in the summer of 1940.

Secrets of the Wyrde Woods: Forgotten Road
(Historical Fantasy, summer 1940)

Maisy Robbins is evacuated from her beloved London for her safety and sent to live with her grandparents in the Sussex Weald. Adjusting to her new environment is hard at first, but Maisy wouldn't be Maisy if she didn't manage to land herself into all sorts of trouble before too long. Hooking up with a new friend, local girl Joy Whitfield, Maisy begins to uncover some of the many secrets of the Wyrde Woods.

Secrets of the Wyrde Woods: Hidden Spring
(Historical Fantasy, spring 1941 – due in 2021/2022)

It's a time of discovery for Joy Whitfield, Maisy Robbins, and Will Maskall. Joy starts her training to become a Guardian of the Wyrde Woods, while Maisy and Will have to find their own paths in order to play their part in the ongoing Wyrde Woods saga.

238

Extract from *Will's War in Brighton*

*(Will and Brenda's experiences during the Brighton Blitz in
the summer of 1940 preceding Will's War in Exile.)*

Deep zigzag trenches had been cut into the playground behind the school and the children piled in quite casually after noting the sky was devoid of the sight or sound of aircraft. The boys put on their gas masks immediately, half filling the trenches with otherworldly creatures that had strange snouts and large eyes which bulged sideways. The girls were slower, they hated the gas masks because most had shoulder length hair and found the gas masks a nightmare to get off. It was the only time that Brenda was pleased that her family couldn't afford to take her to a hairdresser's. Her mousy hair was much shorter on account of her basin hairstyle, so-called because a pudding basin was upturned and placed on her head every now and then after which Mum would snip off any hair that protruded below the rim. Brenda retrieved her gasmask from the rectangular carton box she carried it in and slipped it over her head.

During the first air raid warning at school it had taken the boys less than a minute to discover that their voices sounded oddly hollow in their new gasmasks and that great fun could be had making funny noises in the masks. The teaching staff were oddly tolerant to the malarkey in the trenches, even when fart sounds had joined the repertoire. Brenda presumed that this was because they could all be torn into a thousand pieces for King and Country if and when the Luftwaffe did make an appearance one day. The trenches would be a death trap in the case of a direct hit she had overheard some teachers tell each other.

"We'll be buggered proper if Jerry knows what he is doing," one of the boys near Brenda said.

She frowned; she had ended up in a part of the trench where her form bordered that of older children. Brenda didn't quite know what 'buggered' meant but she was sure it wasn't polite language. The boy had dark hair but his face was already hidden by his gas mask. He was talking to another lad who had a basin hairstyle just like Brenda, though his hair was almost golden.

Brenda recognized them then. The dark haired one was Jamie, his family lived just a few doors away from her own. The other one was his mate Will, the two were usually inseparable. She shouldn't have really liked them for they were always finding ways of getting in trouble but they sometimes let Eddie play in their games and that was nice.

"That fancy Roedean School for girls has proper ones, I heard." Will answered. "Deep ones girdled with steel like the inside of the rocket ships in the pictures. We ought to sneak in one day and have a peek, Jamie."

Brenda crossed her eyes; one advantage of the gasmasks was that nobody could see your facial expression very well and it seemed the only suitable response for the idiocy of boys. They weren't going to take Eddie along on that expedition, she would see to it.

"What if there's an air raid?" Jamie asked. "We'd be stuck in them tunnels with a bunch of girls, Will. Hours on end. We'll both go bloody daft."

"True," Will answered. "Girls are silly."

Brenda glared at them both. She was standing quite close to them but they hadn't noticed it was her.

"Bbbrrrpppfffttt." Jamie blew a raspberry in his mask and within seconds their trench sounded like all the boys suffered from a collective attack of dysentery. Brenda joined the other girls in shaking her head in exasperation. She suspected that one or two girls happily joined in as it was difficult to tell who was making what specific noise when so many were at it. Classes had grown somewhat with the induction of evacuee children from London and some of those could be quite rude, or so Brenda thought. The teacher in charge of this section of the trench, Mr. Burchell, shook his head too but made no attempt to stop the fun.

Brenda smiled beneath her mask; the trench games were more fun than lessons and in a way the rude noises were funny. Her smile faded though when she registered the distant drone of plane engines and the pupils became quiet as eyes turned skywards. Some of the more timid children hugged the trench walls. The seagulls wheeling above the school screamed collectively in response to the strange sound of aeroplane engines coming closer at low altitude.

Perhaps a few of the gulls were also startled by the trench which presented an odd sight as hundreds of gas-masked faces were turned upwards. The strange robotic faces looked left and right. They sought to spot the incoming aircraft but it was as if they were shaking a desperate 'no' to whatever danger might be preying on them in the clouds overhead.

When the drone developed into a roar that drowned out the seagulls the nay-saying stopped. Everybody crouched down and made themselves as small as possible. Brenda pressed her side against the trench wall and pulled her knees up to the ventilator of her mask. She hoped Eddie would be alright.

Extract from *Forgotten Road*

(The Wyrde Woods adventures of Maisy and Joy in the summer of 1940, before the arrival of Will Maskall.)

"Joy!" Maisy whispered urgently but her friend remained deep in sleep. Maisy lit a candle and then began to gently shake Joy. "Wake up, Joy. Nommus! Wake up."

Joy opened her eyes and grunted. "Maisy, I was dreaming. A nice dream twere too."

A brief smile of recollection was followed by a frown as Joy peered at Maisy questioningly.

"There is an intruder, ain't it?" Maisy hissed. "A bloody Tea Leaf."

"What?" Joy rose to prop herself on her elbows. "Tea Leaf?"

"A burglar! I can hear him! Downstairs he is. We should go whack him on the head, ain't it?"

"Maisy," Joy shook her head. "The owls…"

"Not the owls," Maisy shook her head. "Listen!"

Joy inclined her head and started hearing the sounds Maisy was referring to. Something was moving about downstairs; bumping into furniture and muttering when it did.

"Oh, that's just Master Dobbs," Joy shrugged. "If it were bad the owls would have made a gurt big stir, Maisy. You can count on that."

"Master who?" Maisy frowned. She had not realised the Owlery had another occupant. "A man?"

The intruder burped loudly.

Joy giggled. "Not quite a man."

They both tilted their heads when Maisy's intruder started singing boisterously.

"Oak's Acorn! We left the mead out, didnt we?" Joy grinned.

"He's lush?" Maisy smirked.

"Only needs the one sip," Joy explained. "Master Dobbs ain't used to much."

"Who the heck is Master Dobbs?"

"Master Dobbs is Farisee," Joy said. "He does chores for us at night."

"Farisee?" Maisy shook her head in confusion.

"A Pook. Faere Folk," Joy said patiently. "The Fae."

"You mean a faery?" Maisy was incredulous.

"They don't like that name," Joy shook her head. "You maun use it, Maisy."

"Are you telling me there's a blooming faery in your living room?" Maisy sounded outraged.

"You maun use that middling name," Joy insisted. "You don't want to upset them, sureleye. I told you the woods were filled with critters of all sorts."

246

Maisy did remember but was not expecting a faer…a Farisee to be rummaging around in the Owlery. Something Joy was casual and matter-of-fact about.

"Back to sleep, Maisy," Joy smiled reassuringly and settled back down. "Mayhap I can still catch that dream."

Still speechless Maisy saw her friend close her eyes in total unconcern. Maisy pinched out the candle and settled on her back. She stared at the darkness above her listening to Master Dobbs continue to potter through the living room below.

Come buy, come buy:
Our grapes fresh from the vine,
Pomegranates full and fine,
Taste them and try:
Currants and gooseberries,
Bright-fire-like barberries,
Figs to fill your mouth,
Citrons from the South,
Sweet to tongue and sound to eye;
Come buy, come buy.

"Just a Pook," Maisy whispered to no one in particular and rolled her eyes.